The Tempting Taste of Danger

by CeeCee James

333~Dedicated to my darling family~333

The only thing worse than a noisy bookstore is patrons literally dying to get out.

Elise Pepper has landed her dream job at the Capture the Magic bookstore. Peace and quiet and thousands of books to herself – including a two million first edition of *Alice in Wonderland*. What more could she ask for?

It can't last of course. Her blissful solitude is rudely interrupted when someone turns the second floor of the building into a Down the Rabbit Hole-themed escape room.

But the noise is the least of her worries – what's worse is the dead bank executive upstairs and the missing first edition. Now Elise is suspected of both theft and murder. Can she find out who did it before she takes the fall for the crime?

Table of Contents

Chapter One

**When the Cuckoo strikes one,
prepare to come undone.
From these pages will crawl
magic to conquer all.**

Elise read the handwritten sign that hung slightly askew on the front door of the Capture the Magic bookstore. She blinked hard, her hand hesitating on the doorknob.

Taking a step back, she glanced along the length of the long building of what had once been a 19th-century mercantile store. She'd always loved this old building. A trickle of apprehension built between her shoulder blades as she anticipated what she was about to do. She wiggled her shoulders against the muscle tension.

Relax. What could possibly happen here?

If she could get through the interview, this job was sure to be a lot safer than her last one. This was a bookstore. No one ever found any dead bodies in bookstores, did they?

Straightening herself to her full five foot, four inches height, Elise swiftly twisted the knob and opened the door. Her steps were purposeful as she strode inside.

Not three steps in, one of her high-heeled shoes caught on the welcome mat and nearly sent her sprawling. Her gasp echoed in the store. Somewhat abashed, she tried to garner up her confidence again as she walked across the dark, pitted wood floor.

The scent of books surrounded her and brought a calming effect. Taking a deep breath, she savored the soft smell of paper, binding, and ink under the note of coffee. A smile crossed her lips. *This is it. I think I've found my dream job.*

Rows of books were arranged laterally on large wooden shelves. Colorful signs hung over each aisle with the description of the genre in the same scrawling print as the sign on the door.

From the back of the shop came the sound of a cappuccino machine. She paused for a moment to find the source of the noise. There it was, on the far side of the travel section. A cute coffee bar had been set up, including a counter with stools and a glass case filled with treats. Three round tables with chairs sat cozied between the bar and two red, velvety couches.

A man behind the bar waved as he caught her eye. Looking to be in his early thirties—the same age as Elise—he had dark scruffy hair and wore a comfortable-looking blue flannel shirt. He pushed thick-framed glasses up his nose with a finger and smiled—a nice smile. He was handsome, but not as handsome as Brad, her boyfriend.

"You're right on time for the interview. I just wanted to give you a second to acclimate before I called you over," he said, setting a white mug of coffee on the counter. "Coffee?"

"Yes, please!" Elise smiled back and walked over there. She winced slightly at how loud her heels sounded in the room.

"Cream or sugar?" He came around from behind the bar and extended his hand. "By the way, my name's David McCall. You can call me Dave. I'm the owner here."

"Hi, Dave." Elise gratefully took his hand. It was still warm from holding the coffee. After a few shakes, he reached for the mug and handed it to her, and then nodded in the direction of the cream and sugar at the end of the bar. She waited as he walked back behind the counter and grabbed his own mug. This one was obviously his personal cup, with a wicked smiley face complete with horns that said "World's Best Boss."

"Nice." she gestured. "Should I be worried?"

He chuckled. "Well, my last employee got this for me right before he disappeared."

"Disappeared?" she asked as they walked toward the condiments.

"Yeah. They're still looking for the body."

Elise paused, feeling slightly chilled.

At the look on her face, he chuckled again. "I'm kidding. I'm kidding. Capture the Magic bookstore...." He motioned with his hand. "Poof!"

"Ahh!" Elise smiled. "Funny." She reached for the sugar packets and took two. Shaking them, she continued. "Do you do magic?"

"I do magic every day." His face became serious. "Every time I sell a book. I offer adventure to the housebound, love and romance to the lonely, heroes for those who need vindication, and laughs for those with no one to joke with." He took a sip of his coffee, then looked at her with his brow wrinkled. "So yes, I guess you could say I'm a magician."

"I'd never thought of books that way before. But you're right. I've escaped into them many times."

"Exactly." His face creased into a ready smile. Obviously, it was something he did frequently, as the many lines framing his eyes attested. "Poof!" he motioned again. Then, nodding to the rest of the store, he continued. "So, what do you think?" His face showed no outward emotion but his brown eyes sparkled with apparent pride.

Elise glanced around again, this time taking a moment to really study it. The ceilings were dark, lined with the same aged wood as the floors and walls. Hundreds of teacup sized lights hung from circular wagon wheel shaped chandeliers. It gave the business a warm glow and the ambiance of a cozy barn. She could almost imagine hay bales and musicians filing out from behind the shelves with fiddles for a barn dance.

She had no qualms with her answer. "I positively love it."

Dave grinned again, seeming to appreciate her enthusiasm. "Me too. This place used to be my grandma's. Not many people dream of owning a bookstore, but it's been mine since I was a little kid. I used to come here after school and sit right over there." He pointed to an alcove by the window. "And Grandma would bring over a pile of the newest train books, or pick your own adventures, and I'd read all afternoon until my mom came to pick me up after work." He took another sip of coffee, his eyes still studying the bench. "I had no idea she was babysitting me. I thought I was helping grandma run the store."

"Aw," Elise smiled. It immediately warmed her up to him even more.

"Yeah, when she died, she left all of this to me. Most people live a life they need a vacation from. Me, I live a life where I truly love what I do." He turned his attention back to her. "Pretty lucky, huh?"

Elise nodded slowly and took another sip of the coffee. A flicker of excitement started building inside of her. *This could be your life, too!*

"So," Dave's voice took a hint of professionalism. "Your last place of employment was at Wedding Dreams?"

Elise felt her face flush as she nodded. *Oh no....*

"That's the one where the owner went to jail?"

She gave another nod, resisting the urge to bite her lip.

His eyebrows furrowed curiously. "And, are you the one that found the cake decorator.... Dead?"

Her bottom lip found it's way into her mouth as she gave the barest of nods. Finding dead bodies was not a skill she wanted on her resume, let alone talk about during an interview.

Dave's face wrinkled into a look of sympathy. "Aw, man. I'm so sorry. That must have been traumatic for you. And yet, look at you now." The corner of his lip lifted into a half-smile. "Ready for the next adventure. You're a trooper. I like that."

Relief flooded through Elise and she breathed out. "Thank you. It's something I'd sooner forget."

"So, things here at the bookstore go at a much slower pace than I assume wedding planning does. It might be downright boring. You sure you're okay with that?"

"Absolutely. After my last job, the word *boring* is like music to my ears."

"Your job will be to man the coffee bar and cash register. Keep things tidy. And in your downtime, read. Seriously. I want you to brush up on all the classics as well as the new releases because part of your job will be to understand what the patron is looking for. What they need." His eyes grew a bit introspective. "Sometimes they just want entertainment, and sometimes what they really need is a book to change their life. They might not even know what they want." He locked his eyes with hers. "Your job will be to figure it out for them."

Elise nodded, a little more slowly this time.

"Now, come on. Let me show you the shop's pride and joy." As if hit by a bolt of electricity, he set the cup down and strode across the room. Elise followed, her heels clacking.

There, in the center of the room, stood a glass case on a waist-high pedestal. Resting on a white silk pillow inside sat an old book. Elise leaned closer to read the title. *Alice's Adventures in Wonderland* by Lewis Carrol. The book was in pristine condition. The dark book cover, illustrated with a little girl sitting under a tree, showed no wear on its corners. Next to the book was a metal plaque that stated— 1865 First Edition.

"Wow! That's incredible," Elise said, suitably impressed. "I've never seen anything like it before."

Dave gazed at the book with a look of adoration, the light reflecting off the glass case casting a light glow on his face. "Two point one million dollars," he murmured.

"Excuse me?" Elise said, slightly shocked.

He lifted his head to look at her. "What you see there is two-point-one-million dollars. A gift given to my great-grandmother by Lewis Carrol, himself."

Elise felt her jaw drop. "You're kidding me." She studied it again, this time eyeing the glass case. "And you just have it sitting out here? No alarm or anything?"

Dave shrugged. "Our building has an alarm. And there's a camera over there." He pointed to an opposite corner.

"This is kind of ironic. I once tried out for an *Alice in Wonderland* play in high school."

"Really?" His eyes lit up.

"Yeah. Actually auditioned for the part of Alice. My hair was lighter then. Those were my Sun-In days," she joked.

"Sun-In?" he looked confused.

"It's a hair lightener. Never mind. Anyway, I missed out on Alice, but they did let me do some stage decorating."

"Oh. yeah?" He smiled. "Get a lot of painting experience?"

"Just one thing. A mushroom for the caterpillar. The thing was, I was so slow that it took me all week to finish. Oddly, they let me go after that." She shook her head at the memory. "Don't worry. I'm much faster now."

"Unless I ask you to paint."

"Yeah. I guess that's true." She grinned. "Anyway, I can't believe you have something so priceless just sitting out here."

"Well, not too many people know what this book is worth. Just my family. The odd book connoisseur." Dave smiled at her. "And now you."

Chapter Two

"So," Dave reached out his hand to Elise for the second handshake of the day. "Let's make it official. You're hired."

Elise shook his hand, attempting to appear responsible, as she stifled a junior-high squeal of excitement. "Awesome! I'm looking forward to it."

"Any more questions?"

"Well, where do those stairs go to over there?" She pointed to a staircase near the entrance.

"Those lead to the second floor." He grinned as Elise rolled her eyes. "Actually, that's where my grandparents used to live. Upstairs used to be a full apartment, and there's actually a second set of stairs back there." He jabbed his index finger in the direction of a closed door at the back of the room. "There's a sign on the door that says 'broom closet' so the customers don't get it mixed up with the restroom. It used to say "caution, live monsters, spiders and snakes," but too many people were curious." He grinned at his own joke. "I had so many people up that stairwell I should have charged admission."

"Count me off that list. So what's up there now? Is that where you live?"

He shook his head. "Nah. I have a townhome down at Meadow Heights. As much as I love the bookstore, I need my quiet space." A shy expression flickered over his face as he glanced to the ground. "Actually, I'm a writer, too. Or aspiring to be."

"Really? That's awesome. What do you write?"

Dave grinned again. That smile never seemed far away. "Don't freak out." He raised an eyebrow as if daring her.

"I promise. I won't freak out. Seriously, I admire anyone who can get their thoughts out on paper. I have a hard enough time just getting them out of my mouth."

"Well, I don't know how great the words are, but I write horror."

Elise raised her eyebrows. "Horror, huh? So the monsters, snakes and spiders might have been a real thing."

"Yeah," he laughed again. "Lots of dead bodies. Bloody chopped-off limbs."

Elise felt a coil of unease at the thought of chopped-off body parts. *Okay. I'm freaked out.* For the first time since she'd met Dave, she got something other than a warm feeling when she met his eyes. But had it been him or just the mention of chopped off body parts that had a shiver building in the base of her spine?

A bang came from the stairwell. Elise jumped and spun to look.

"Oh. Don't worry." Dave held out a hand to steady her. "It's not a chainsaw murderer coming to get us. Just one of the construction workers."

Elise laughed louder than needed to cover her startled reaction. She clenched her hands together to hide the adrenaline shake. "Construction workers? What's going on?"

"Yeah. A few months ago I rented the apartment space. It's actually been kind of weird sharing the building." His hand slid off her arm. He shifted awkwardly and jammed it into his pocket. "I'm kind of a loner except for my customers."

"And your missing employee," Elise teased, half-waiting for real assurance that the guy was okay.

Dave chuckled. "Him too. Although he still stops by from time to time. All of his limbs intact."

Elise laughed, having been caught fishing for information. "So what about this rental?"

"Uh, yeah." He cleared his throat. "Anyway, a group of entrepreneurial college kids have rented the space for their business. They're building an escape room."

"Oh," Elise tried to look like she knew what he was talking about. "Really. How interesting."

"You have no idea what I'm talking about, do you?"

Caught again! "Nope!" Elise shrugged. "Tell me what it is. Sounds interesting."

"It's a game. They lock you in the room, and you have to use a series of clues to solve different puzzles to find your way out."

"Sounds...lovely," Elise deadpanned. *This place was getting weirder and weirder.*

Dave chuckled. "Not your thing?"

"Depends. I'm an ace at the Game of Life. Monopoly not so much."

"This is more like a maze, or a game of Clue. You have to figure out the clues, and then use them to solve the puzzle." He shrugged. "I don't know, I think it sounds pretty cool. I thought they were already done, so I'm surprised to hear more construction going on."

"So, they're not open then?"

"I heard the grand opening's going to be soon. I think they're going to let me test it out. I aim to break it." He grinned mischievously. "I'm really good at these things."

"I'm surprised people really pay to do these things. Get locked up in a room and all."

"Yeah," Dave nodded. "These Escape rooms are popping up all over the place with different themes. Some have 'Steal the Mona Lisa', some have 'Escape the Murderer.' One's 'Steal the Crown Jewels.' This one here is called 'Escape down the Rabbit Hole.'" He smiled. "Their nod to our *Alice in Wonderland* book."

"Oh, that's kind of neat. So it must be Alice in Wonderland themed?"

"I don't know. I'm guessing so." He tipped his head and gave her another shy smile. "Want to come with me when I check it out?"

"Okay. Sure. That does sound kind of interesting."

He wrinkled his nose. "Kind of?"

"Well, I'll admit, I'm not much of a game person. And, I'm half-afraid I'd be locked in there for good." She shot him a worried look. "They do let you out eventually, right?"

"No, they keep you locked in there and let the bodies pile up." He laughed. "Of course they let you out. I think they give you an hour to solve the riddles and clues."

"I knew that. The thought of being locked up just causes an irrational fear, I guess."

"Yeah, that's the point. To get passed the fear and win the game. No one wants to be rescued."

"When is it going to be ready?"

Loud clumping came down the stairs. "Let's ask the man of the hour himself," Dave answered.

A young man with red hair hanging in his face tromped down the stairs. He wore a carpenter's belt around his baggy jeans, and the handle of the hammer banged against his leg with every step.

"Hey, Dave!" he called, brushing the hair out of his eyes. "How's it going?"

"Jake! I was just going to ask you the same thing. How are things up there?"

"Oh, it's going good. We should be ready for the tour tomorrow." He scratched his nose, bringing Elise's attention to his many freckles.

"This is Elise. She's going to be our new shopkeeper."

Jake looked at his hand first then brushed it off on the back of his pants. He thrust it out to Elise. "Hi, there. I'm Jake. Nice to meet you."

Elise noticed his arm was heavily covered with freckles as well. "It's nice to meet you," she responded, shaking his hand. "Escape from the Rabbit hole, huh?" she flicked her gaze toward the second story.

"Out of the rabbit hole, and yeah. It's pretty cool. You'll have to come see it sometime."

"I'd love too. I guess I'm accompanying Dave."

"Oh, cool." The young man nodded. "Well, I'm just off to pick up a few more things. Wires, lightbulbs. The hardware manager knows me by name," he joked. "I'll catch you guys later."

They waved as he headed out the door.

"He and his partner are both pretty nice guys. I think this is going to work out really well. Hopefully, their customers will want to hang out here for a bit, waiting for their turn to go through the room." He glanced at her. "I'll take all the business I can get, now that ebooks have eaten into my trade."

Elise nodded. "Maybe you could have a section by the stairs that just focuses on mysteries. Or games? Maybe comic books?" she threw out, trying to hit all the markets.

He tapped his chin with his index finger. "I like the way you think. I knew there was a reason why I hired you."

Chapter Three

It was the start of her second week there — each day easier than the last as she learned her way around the coffee shop and bookstore — that Elise opened the bookstore to see three men talking at the bottom of the stairs. Dave she recognized, but the other two were new to her.

"Hey, hey! There she is!" Dave gave his characteristic big grin. His arm reached around her, eventually coming to rest on her upper back. "Elise, this is Thomas, the other side of the brain-trust of the Escape room." A young man with sandy-blond hair stuck out his hand. Elise shook it quickly.

"And this is Harry," Dave continued.

"He's the brawn to our brains," Thomas volunteered.

"Oh, really?" Elise said, her hand outstretched. Harry was tall, much taller than the rest of them, bald, and about her age. Still, he was in excellent shape, and his muscles flexed under his shirt as he took her hand. Elise felt like a little girl as she looked up. "The brawn, huh? It's nice to meet you."

"Nice to meet you too." His eyes were the color of hot chocolate and his voice deep and low. Releasing her hand, he gave her a warm smile, showing two dimples.

"I'm the head contractor of this shin-dig." He glanced up the stairs. "Been one of the most interesting projects I've ever done, to say the least."

"I can only imagine how fun it was, making traps to escape from and expecting customers to pay to be the mice. And all of it in honor of the store's Alice in Wonderland book." She smiled at him again before her gaze flicked over to her boss. "I guess we're getting a tour today, huh Dave?"

"Are you guys sure this time? Because you've told me 'tomorrow' about five times already." he answered, looking at Thomas and Jake. "Am I right, boys?"

"Quit giving us a hard time and let's go put those reasoning skills to the test." Thomas grinned cheekily.

Elise arched an eyebrow at Thomas confidently, even though her insides quaked at the thought of being locked in a room. No windows. No way out.

Harry gave her the thumbs up. "Don't let me down, now."

She nodded with stoicism, even as her ankles felt weak as she climbed the stairs. *People do this for fun. It's a challenge.* Taking a shaky grab, she grabbed the door jam. *I can do this.* "All right, let's go." The words fell from her mouth with zero enthusiasm.

"Hey. You going to be okay going in there?" Thomas's eyebrows rose in concern at her expression. "Don't break anything. Don't take anything off the walls. The things needing to be unlocked or solved aren't going to require anything over your head to be taken down. Or ripped off the wall." He eyed her again as she gave him a thumbs up. Nodding, he continued. "You've got sixty minutes." He glanced at his watch. "Starting now."

Thomas opened the door and ushered them in. As the door was closing, he yelled, "And be careful of the—"

The door clicked shut.

"Be careful?" Elise's stomach rolled with nausea. Not the words she wanted to hear in a near-pitch black room. She looked at Dave. Things were easy between them, but she usually worked at the store alone. It was a bit odd to be locked in a room with him.

Dave mumbled. "He probably just said that to make us more tense. Okay. Let's go."

It took a moment for Elise's eyes to adjust to the room and absorb the surroundings. Neon-colored lights made the psychedelic swirls of color in the darkness. There were mini-stations along the wall. Pipes and drawers and a book on a table and a peg board. A life-size illustrated Grandfather clock, crazy eyes, and dancing mushrooms competed for the visual palette along with strings of wires, blinking lights, and rows of boxes.

Sweat accumulated at the base of Elise's neck. She lifted up her hair. "What do we do now?"

"Well, now we look for the question."

"Question?"

"Yeah, to show us which puzzle to solve first."

They wandered around the room studying the panels on the wall. Elise noticed the floor where a yellow painted arrow pointed to a massive spinning wheel—like a roulette wheel—that hung from the wall.

"Clue number one," she said.

The wheel hung under a clear pipe, obviously waiting for something to fall from the pipe to make the wheel spin. All around it was painted glowing eyes that stared at them. Elise's gaze followed the pipe as it traveled away from the wheel. Fake vines draped from the wall and partially covered it, but she could see where the pipe curved around onto the corner and ended above a large chest.

Dave noticed it at the same time she did. The glanced at each other and both walked over.

"What do you think of this?" he asked. He fiddled with the chest, trying to open it. It remained locked.

She felt herself loosening up. *I can totally do this.* The challenge of the games suddenly seemed fun.

The top of the chest held a book—the encyclopedia of all things about *Alice in Wonderland*—and the wall above it had a peg board. Colored pegs could be used to connect a string from one picture to another. After a few moments, they concluded that the pegs coordinated with answers in the book. Quickly, they looked up the answers and placed the pegs in their correct spots on the board.

When the last peg was placed, a small door popped open on the front of the chest. They grinned at each other.

It revealed a key. A key to what? Eventually, the trail took them over to another game where they had to guess the different color combination to imitate the swirls of smoke coming off a painted hookah pipe. The answer to that revealed a locked box. They opened it with their key and discovered a ladle. After finishing another puzzle, they found a vase with a ping-pong ball at the bottom.

Still another game led them to a source of water. The ladle finally made sense as it came into use transporting the water to fill the vase until the ping pong ball floated to the surface and they were able to grab it.

Finally, they took the ball to the clear pipe. Elise held the ball to the end and the pipe sucked it up, much like the machine at the bank drive-through.

They followed the ball as it traveled around the room in its pipe until it was finally spit out onto the wheel.

The wheel clicked as it spun. When it stopped the ball fell into a numbered slot. A small drawer popped open on the table underneath.

Elise and Dave leaned over curiously. Inside the drawer sat a plate with two pink-frosted cookies on it.

The note next to it said- **Take a bite and go small.**

Elise eyed the cookies on the plate. "Um. No." She crossed her arms with a decided frown.

"What? It's no big deal. We have to figure this out." Dave turned the plate with his finger.

"You go for it. I'm not eating any of this. Hello, A." She lifted a finger to number her points, "We don't know who touched that or where they came from."

"Maybe out of a cookie package?"

"They look homemade." She glanced at them again. "Who knows what they're made with."

"It's the adventure," Dave said, picking up the cookie.

Elise read the sign again. "Wait a second. Something's wrong here. In *Alice in Wonderland*, doesn't the drink make her shrink, and the food make her grow? This is the opposite." She shook her head. "We have to be missing a clue."

"So, you don't think we should eat it?" Dave's eyebrows rumpled.

"Eat it if you want, but that's not the game. It's just the clue." She examined the wheel, searching for something.

"What are you looking for?"

"Opposites. Strong opposites," Elise muttered. *Short, tall, big small.*

The painted grandfather clock on the wall was the tallest thing in the room. She walked over and studied it again.

Something behind the wheel began a series of long beeps. The beeps grew louder and closer together. Elise felt her pulse ramp up along with it.

Next to her, Dave's movements became more erratic as the noise affected him too.

"What about this?" he asked, pointing to the clock's face.

The numbers were mixed-up. Instead of a twelve being at the top, it was a six. She stared at the clock then dropped to a knee.

The pendulum was a circle box with a real punch-code lock. Words painted around it said, "The chime at the top and Under the bottom."

Top of the hour is six. She punched in the number. It turned green, leaving the other two spaces blank.

She read the code again. **Under the bottom.** Whirling, she raced to the plate of cookies and picked it up. Nothing. She flipped the plate over. Relief flooded through her at the sight of number—93.

Back at the lock, she typed in 39. All three lights turned green and a click was heard. The painted edge of the clock cracked, revealing a door.

"How did you know to flip the numbers around?" Dave said, sounding impressed.

"The clue said, eat it to go small, so I did the smaller number first." She pushed the panel in the clock to open it wider.

"Very interesting. You should be a detective."

"I like working in a bookstore. It's safer." She smiled. Her grin fell off as flashing lights from the other side of the panel shown through into their room. A groan came out of her. "There's another room?"

He shrugged sheepishly and tugged on his beard. "Yeah. I guess so."

Oh, my word. Elise squeezed her forehead as the first throb of a headache made its warning. "It's taken us forty minutes to get out of the first room. How many rooms are there?"

Dave shook his head. "I've got no idea, but we better get a move on and find out."

Elise wasted no time in the next room. Ignoring the sirens, the flashing lights and the bizarre colors, she studied the walls. *The door has to be around here somewhere.*

There was the obvious door, but once she tried the handle, she found it was locked.

Another part of the wall was covered with a blanket. While Dave fiddled with a maze of matching up color slides, she walked over to the blanket and flipped it up.

Just a plain piece of wood paneling. She pushed on the paneling and smiled at its springiness. Something was behind it. "Dave! Over here!"

He joined her in helping her pry the board off the wall. A door was revealed behind it.

"We did it!" she said, giving Dave a hug. She reached for the knob and squealed with excitement as it turned in her hand. The two of them hurried through the doorway and onto a set of stairs.

"Whoa! Whoa! Whoa!" a male voice yelled. "What the heck did you do?" An incredulous Thomas stared at her from around the corner. "Did you break our room?"

"What do you mean? We won!"

The young man shook his head, eyes wide. "Nope. You were supposed to find that doorway there," he pointed to where Jake stood with a matching look of surprise on his freckled face. "What did you do?"

"I just pushed on the paneling," Elise demonstrated, "And it popped off."

Dave grinned at her. "Boys, I think she's the winner, no matter what you say."

"Well, crap," Thomas sighed. He ran his hands along the open doorway. "Jake, we've got to cover this somehow. And not with a blanket." He shot his friend a scowl. "I should have known that would have never worked."

"I told her not to take anything off the wall."

Elise wrinkled her nose. "Shoot. Everything was popping open. I forgot. I'm sorry."

"No worries. That's what this run through is for," Thomas turned to Jake. "Now, what are we going to do to cover this?

"A painting," his partner suggested. "We'll get one of a giant rabbit or a tea set or something. Relax. It'll be okay."

"Anyway, you were supposed to pull a square puzzle piece out of here," Thomas pointed to a box, "Which fits into there," he jabbed his thumb in the direction of a flashing machine. "Which opened up a box for the key to the doorway over there, leading back down the front stairs."

Elise blinked hard. "I knew that."

Dave laughed. "I thought it was incredible. Great job, guys. I really loved it." He turned to Elise. "Ready to get out of here?"

Elise felt terrible. "Yeah. I really am sorry guys."

The two young men had already turned their attention to fixing their escape room. "No worries. And you did win!"

"Do I get a prize?"

"Yeah!" Thomas yelled. "A cookie."

Dave led the way down the stairs. He opened the door and they both re-entered the bookstore. Elise smiled and took a deep breath at the beautiful sight of the bright rectangles of sunshine on the floor. She looked back at Dave. "Never again," she vowed.

❋ ❋ ❋

On the way home that night, Elise had to stop at the store to pick up a few groceries. Oddly, she was buying ramen noodles once more even though she'd sworn she'd never eat them again. Lucy loved them.

Lucy was the homeless teenager she'd invited to stay with her a few months ago. So far, things had been going pretty smoothly. The girl was easy to please—as the noodles seemed to attest to—and back in school. Things with Brad, Elise's boyfriend, were going great. He was still an officer with the Angel Lake police department and was up for a promotion soon. Life was finally going in the direction she'd always dreamed about.

When she got back out to her car with her groceries, she was annoyed to notice a flyer under her windshield wiper. She hated it when people did that. She popped the hatch on her Pinto and unloaded the few bags from the cart. After returning the cart to the stall, she ripped the paper out.

Her irritation faded and her blood ran cold as she stared at the flyer.

It was a picture of her from the shoulders up.

She remembered when it had happened—just yesterday. She'd been frustrated to discover her towel had not been hanging at its customary place on the rack. Somehow she'd overlooked it was missing when she climbed into the shower and had been forced to run naked and wet through her bedroom to grab her bathrobe.

Who was watching her? She turned it over to read crude printing.

My shy girl- a piece of advice

If you don't want the rest of this picture plastered all over town.

Be prepared to pay the price.

Chapter Four

Elise sighed as she tried to reread the same page in her mystery as she sat at the bookshop for her shift the next day. It was her third time attempting to get through it. Dave had her running the store alone now, but right now being alone was the last thing she wanted. All she could think about was the picture from last night.

She'd shown it to Brad when she'd got home. He'd been understandably incensed, swearing to her, "Baby, I'm going to find that guy." With him being a cop, she had no doubt that he would. He'd taken the picture, clenched in a trembling fist, and walked around the house to find the direction that it had been taken from.

It turned out that there was just enough of a crack between her curtains on her bedroom window to allow a glimpse into her bathroom. She'd promptly covered the window with a blanket that night and planned to purchased blinds on her way home tonight.

The bell jingled above the store's door, the sound barely entering Elise's consciousness as she turned the page in her book.

"Hey! Anyone here?" A male voice caused Elise to look up.

She pasted on her best customer service smile. "Back here!" she called.

The bell dinged again and this time male laughter filled the air. The sound was jarring in the quiet bookstore. Elise set the book under the counter and walked forward to meet the group.

"Shhh," one of the men said, waving his hands to quiet his friends. He was heavy-set, and his face was flushed, with skin the texture of an orange peel. His eyes lit up at the sight of Elise, and he quickly looked down.

"There he goes," his dark-haired buddy said with a smirk, "Catches a sight of a pretty woman and blows up like a puffer fish." To imitate his friend, the dark-haired man puffed his cheeks out and hid his face like he was shy.

"Shut up, Tim!" The first man shoved his friend in the shoulder.

"Leave him alone," a third man said. This one looked a bit more put together than the other two. He straightened his business jacket and pushed up his glasses. "Y'all are hammered. That's what you get for having lunch at Tobacco Johns."

Elise's ears perked at the name of the well-known sports bar. *Lovely. Three drunk men. Wonder what books they'll have me search up?*

"Can I help you?" she asked.

The heavy man gave her a slow appraisal from top to bottom. Elise crossed her arms over her chest and gave him a stern look. He stood unsteadily on his feet.

"Up this way, I guess?" The jacketed man gestured to the stairs..

"This is your idea, Steve. Lead the way." Tim clapped the large man on the back.

"Murder, mayhem and mystery await." The last man said, starting up the stairs.

"What if we can't get out in time?" Steve looked nervous despite the intoxication.

The third man ran his finger across his throat in a dramatic fashion.

Steve pushed him. "Yeah, whatever. Anything happens to me and I'm suing YOU."

Ignoring her, the three of them pounded up the stairs, the heels of their leather dress shoes echoing throughout the bookstore. At the top, Steve tried the knob. It didn't open. He scratched his head as his forehead creased in confusion.

"I guess they don't want us in there, then." He laughed.

"Get out of the way. You don't know the secret knock." Tim pushed the two others out of the way and thumped on the door.

Still no answer.

Elise heard one darkly mutter, "Are you serious? I left the game for this?"

"Just chill out. They're coming." Tim looked at his watch. "We're like two minutes early."

"I can't believe I let you talk me into this," the big guy grumbled.

"Knock it off. It's supposed to be really cool."

Just then, the bell dinged again as the store's door opened, and Jake materialized in the doorway. "Greetings," he said in a formal tone, his flannel shirt buttoned to the neck. "Welcome to the Rabbit Hole." He jogged up the stairs.

One of the guys chuckled.

Jake started in with the game's rules. "If you can get out within sixty minutes you win two hundred dollars. Don't take anything off the walls. Every clue you need will be easily accessible."

"What if we can't get out?" the big guy asked. "After all, we're bankers, not handymen."

"Your funeral." The guy with the glasses smirked again. "And don't lump me in with that. I'm pretty good with my hands."

"At the end of sixty minutes, if you've failed to solve the puzzle, a loud buzzer will sound and the door will automatically open," Jake answered above their bantering.

"Automatically, huh? You're not opening it?" A worried look from Steve.

Jake shook his head. "It's set on a timer."

The men raised their eyebrows as they glanced at each other. Elise could see that the thought of being locked in there, dependent on an automated door, wafted away the last bit of alcohol fumes.

"What about the door knobs?" asked Tim.

Jake shook his head. "Once you're in there, you're stuck. If you have an emergency, there's an intercom on the wall that you can push to contact someone to help you. But only use it if you have an emergency, not just if you have a question."

"What happens if we solve it before the sixty minutes?"

"The door unlocks and the two hundred bucks are yours." Jake unlocked the door and gestured with his hand. "You ready to give it a shot?"

"I don't know, Steve isn't looking so hot about getting locked into a room now," said Tim.

"Shut up," Steve growled. He pulled at his shirt collar and jerked his chin. Then, clenching his arms in a show of bravado, he pushed the door open. "All right. Let's go."

The three men shuffled through the doorway and the door closed with a loud, ominous click behind them.

Having been in there yesterday, Elise knew what they were seeing. The spiraling neon lights, the fluorescent flowers and mushrooms. She'd found it very disconcerting.

After a few moments, she figured they'd probably located the arrow on the floor and was following it. She could hardly wait to see them in an hour. There would be no way they'd be winning the money.

Jake came down the stairs two at a time. "I'm just going to get a quick bite to eat across the street. I'll be watching from the restaurant," he called to her at the door. "Thomas is waiting there with the laptop set up already."

Elise gave him an *okay* sign and meandered back to the coffee station. With a sigh, she pulled out the book again.

I can finish this. It's just one book. I won't let it beat me.

But, just like last time, her mind began to spin. The words ran together across the page.

Bang! An avalanche of thumping came from the last aisle in the store. Startled, Elise jumped from her stool and ran back there. The stack of books she'd just built for a display had fallen from the table and onto the floor.

Darn it. Books lay in piles, some with open faces, some with their spines creased. She stooped to begin gathering them up.

As she piled them back on the table, she heard the bell chime over the entrance again. She scooped up the last few and set them on the table, then walked to the front of the store.

There was no one there.

Brow wrinkled, she meandered through the store, trying to be as unobtrusive as possible as she glanced down each aisle.

Where the heck did they go?

Each aisle was empty—a testament to the slowness on a Tuesday afternoon. *I know I heard that bell.* Chewing her lip, she walked back to the front. *Maybe it was someone who'd wanted a cup of coffee and saw the counter was empty, so they'd left?* Frowning, she returned to the back table and began stacking the books into the display.

Another bang happened. Elise jumped. This one was overhead and she looked up as the muffled thumping continued. *The men must be in the second room now.* Something heavy fell, so hard that dust sifted down from the ceiling. Elise leaped back, her mouth open. *What in the world?*

A wail sounded next, high and unidentifiable. It came again—a scream for help.

She ran for the stairs.

Chapter Five

Elise ran up the stairs and grabbed for the doorknob. She twisted it hard but it wouldn't open. Panic struck her and she slammed her shoulder against the door to jar it loose. On the other side, the men pounded and jerked at the door.

"Help! Help!" they screamed.

"What's going on? I'm trying to get it open!" She yelled, slapping the door.

"Get us out of here!" The wood reverberated under their fists.

Elise took a step back, eyeing the door. She'd never seen it locked from this side before. Suddenly, she remembered the hidden passage and skirted back down the stairs. The men's cries took a desperate note as they heard her retreating steps.

She raced across the bookstore to the door marked "broom closet." With sweat-soaked hands, she wrenched the door open and then pounded up the steps. Her heart felt like it was choking her as she reached the door.

It was quiet up here at the back of the building. Her footfalls sounded loud in the hush, and the men's voices were faint. She twisted the doorknob and felt a flutter of relieved shock as it opened under her hand.

The door still didn't open. She remembered Jake mentioning hanging a picture there and shoved hard. There was a clatter as whatever it was fell to the floor. *Thank God it wasn't tacked well.*

Inside, the room was dark with the exception of the flashing neon lights. The strobe blinking made her sick to her stomach.

She walked inside and waited for her eyes to adjust to the light. Across the room was the other door where the group of men was trapped. She started towards it.

After a few steps, she froze.

A dark shadow blocked the door.

She squinted hard at it, trying to discern what it was. Light flickered over it, showing it to be large and low to the ground.

She gasped when the light flashed on a pale face.

It was Steve.

He was slumped over, his face half-covered by an arm. One of his dress shoes was missing, showing a toe that poked through a hole in his sock. Glancing about, Elise located the shoe about three feet away.

He wasn't moving as she ran to his side.

"Steve? Are you okay?" She grabbed his arm and shook him.

Steve's arm fell limply to his side like a hunk of meat. Elise drew back with a shudder as he stared with sightless eyes.

"No," she whispered as she dug in his neck to feel for a pulse. Nothing. "Steve?" she screamed and shook him harder.

The men in the other room heard her and came pounding on this room's door. Their kicks vibrated through the wood and shook Steve's body resting against it.

Using all her strength, Elise reached under his arms and tried to move him so he could be flat on his back and away from the door. She grunted under his weight. The smell of the man's cologne mixed with the odor of vomit. Holding her breath, she tugged and finally shifted his body a few inches. She opened the door a crack.

One of the men on the other side tried to open it more. Cursing ensued as the door resisted. Like a bulldozer, the men began shoving the door.

"Stop!" Elise screamed. "Steve's right here. You're pushing into him! Call 911!"

"You don't think I already did that?" a panicked voice answered her. "Is he okay?"

The door nudged against Steve's limp form again. Elise used the momentum to help roll the heavy man. Tim was able to squeeze through the crack. Elise positioned Steve's chin up and gave him three quick breaths. Tim knelt to feel for a pulse.

"Nothing!" he called as the other man filed in. Tim began to do CPR on his friend, while the third man with the glasses swept past Elise and ran down the back stairs.

"Come on, Come on," Tim muttered as he compressed Steve's chest. After twenty-five compressions, Elise pinched Steve's nose and gave him two breaths.

The room felt alive with electricity.

Nothing.

Finally, sirens could be heard. Paramedics filed up the back stairs and took over the CPR. They loaded Steve onto a gurney and brought him down the stairs, leaving Elise alone with Tim.

She pushed back to sit on the floor with her face in her hands. Her mouth tasted sour. Never in her life had she felt more tired and sore, even after running the half-marathon.

Tim sat next to her, his head resting against the back wall.

Jake ran up the stairs with Thomas behind him. His eyes were wild. "You guys okay?"

Elise nodded. "Did you see what happened on the camera?"

Thomas shook his head. "No, it went black so we came to see what was wrong. Saw the ambulance here…." he trailed, off, his eyes wide with terror. Elise could only imagine that they were worried about how exactly the guy got hurt at their business.

As the two young men went back down the stairs, Elise heard Jake say, "I can't believe that just happened."

I hear you. Did that just happen? Elise glanced at Tim, who looked equally as shocked. "I'm so sorry." She reached out to touch his elbow. "You did a great job."

Tim rubbed his hands through his hair and stared blankly down the stairwell. "Yeah. You did, too."

"Your friend is going to be okay." Deep in her heart, Elise knew that was a lie. She'd seen Steve's eyes and recognized that look.

"I hope so." He didn't seem to believe it either. "Come on. Let's get out of here."

They both walked down the stairs, meeting a police officer on his way up. The officer turned and headed back down, and the group of them convened at the bottom of the stairs.

Outside, the ambulance took off. Elise noticed the lack of siren with a sinking feeling.

Tim shoved his hands into his pockets. The third guy with the glasses stood staring at the floor, looking lost and dazed.

Jake and Thomas waited in one corner with an officer. Another officer walked up to Elise. He held a pad of paper, and two frown lines formed on either side of his mouth. "Can you give me a few words about what happened up there?"

"Uh, yeah." Tim began. "We were doing the puzzles — we'd actually just finished the one at the table — and the door opened. Steve went through. Then, just like that, the door shut as if it were controlled. Brian and I were locked in on the other side."

"We heard Steve yell for help." Brian's face paled as he interjected.

"Yeah. He yelled for help, and then there was a loud bang. It sounded like he'd fallen. I tried the door. Brian tried the other. We were trapped. We started banging for help and called 911."

"And when did you come into this?" the officer asked Elise.

"I heard them yelling and ran to open the door."

"You ran that way?" The officer indicated the back stairway with his pen.

"Yes, when I couldn't get the main door to open."

"How did you know about that back stairwell?" The officer raised his eyebrows.

"My boss showed it to me on my first day on the job here." Elise was curious at the suspicious tone the officer used.

"Hmmm," the officer gave Elise a steely look, making her feel even more uncomfortable. "So, you were down here alone the entire time while they were up there?"

"Well, I work here." Elise shrugged as a way of explanation.

"Do you know if this place has any security cameras?"

"Just one that I know of," Elise said.

"Do you know where to access the video?"

Elise nodded. "It's in the back room. It downloads to Dave's computer."

"Where does this camera focus?"

"On the bookstore's main attraction. Over there." Elise pointed.

The officer took a few steps in the direction Elise indicated. "Over here? Is it pointed at that?" His mouth turned down even more with apparent skepticism.

Elise followed to show him the book stand.

She gasped. The glass on the display case was smashed and lay in pieces on the ground. The book was gone.

Just then, the officer's mic squawked with a code. He frowned as he answered back. Turning to the two men, his face wore a sympathetic look. He took a deep breath and addressed them both. "I'm sorry. It seems they were not able to resuscitate your friend. They've coded him DOA."

❀ ❀ ❀

Dave arrived soon after and closed the bookstore as the police conducted their investigation. Jake and Thomas sat slumped with depression on the bottom steps of the staircase. An officer reviewed the surveillance video from Dave's computer, while others were upstairs searching the Escape room that was now cordoned off with yellow tape.

After the officer's questions were answered, Dave walked Elise out to her car, past the many police cars. His face seemed to hang even longer with misery at the sight of them blocking his store.

The two of them stopped at her car.

"How are you really doing?" she asked as she rummaged through her purse for her keys. *He'd been saying he's okay but poor guy. A murder in his store and his family heirloom stolen.*

"Honestly, I—I'm a little shocked," he said, his mouth set into two grim lines. He rubbed his beard and hmmmed.

Elise nodded, feeling very discombobulated herself as thoughts pinged around. "Hang in there, okay?"

Yeah, don't worry about me. He clapped her on the back. "All right, unless you hear from me, I'll see you tomorrow." After giving a wave, he walked back inside.

Elise started her car and sighed. She rubbed her thumb against her fingers. *That's weird.* There as an oily residue on her hands. *What in the world did I get into?* She held it to her nose but it didn't have a scent. Frowning, she found a napkin from the glove box and wiped her hands. *All right. I need a long hug and an even longer bath. Please, Brad. Answer your phone.*

Chapter Six

The next morning, Elise felt like time was moving in slow motion. Everything she did, she ended up having to redo again. She grabbed for her hair brush only to drop it twice. Her sneakers kept untying. The cat food bag split down the middle when she picked it up, scattering kibble across the kitchen floor. Later, when she spilled her cereal, she decided to give up on trying on having a normal morning and just headed straight to work.

As she locked her door, she noticed her new neighbors were both outside. They'd just rented the house a few weeks earlier. She'd been meaning to meet them, even had a package of cupcakes she'd bought as a welcome present, but time, as usual, kept getting away from her. She glanced at her watch and, with a sigh, she ran back inside for the treats.

Feeling a bit awkward and in a rush, Elise walked across the street with the plastic container. The neighbors were busy in their garage. The scent of freshly mowed grass hung in the air.

"Hi," Elise said, trying not to startle them. She sounded more chipper than her morning had made her feel. "I'm Elise. I'm your new neighbor."

The dark haired woman looked up from where she was crushing cardboard packing boxes. "Hi, I'm Linda." The young woman reached out her hand. "And this is Seth, my husband."

Her husband wandered over from where he'd been moving the trash cans. He wiped off his hand and held it out. "You might not want to shake after I've been hauling those." He indicated the cans.

"No, that's fine." Elise took his hand too. "Welcome to the neighborhood." She remembered the box of cupcakes and held them out.

"Oh, thank you!" Linda said, giving a warm smile as she accepted the container.

"Are you guys getting settled in okay?" Elise asked, noting another pile of empty boxes in the garage.

"Yes. We're nearly done." Linda said. "I've discovered we're a bunch of packrats. I really can't believe we had so much stuff."

"It's been a huge job, and I'm so over it. I never want to move again," her husband added. He smiled at his wife. "But it was worth it for the fresh start."

Linda nodded in agreement, smiling up at him. "We've moved here because our counselor recommended it. For that new beginning, like Seth was saying."

Elise felt her eyebrows flicker. *Too much information.* "Well, I'm sure you'll love it here. It's a quiet neighborhood, and we all look out for each other."

"Sounds amazing!" Linda said.

"Okay, well I have to get going." Elise took a few steps back. "I just wanted to have a chance to introduce myself."

The three of them said their goodbyes, and Elise waved before heading to her car.

She paused before she climbed inside the Pinto. "Elise in Wonderland" was written in the dust on the side.

Maybe normally she would've laughed at that, but with yesterday's crime and the picture of her, it gave her the chills. She snapped a picture of it with her cell phone. Not sure if she'd need it, but it was better to be safe than sorry. Then, she climbed into her car for a napkin and wiped it clean.

❃ ❃ ❃

Dave was on the phone when she arrived. "She just came through the door. You want to talk to her?" He beckoned her over, his forehead creased with stress.

Elise glanced around the store, tripping out a bit about all that had happened yesterday. What a difference twenty-four hours can make. Really, anything can happen in a day, she noted grimly.

Sighing, she reached for the phone. A jolt of alarm shot through her when she saw Dave's expression as he passed it over. He appeared as though he were sending her to the principal's office.

"Hello?" she said, trying to keep the nervous twinge out of her voice.

"Miss Pepper?" The voice was commanding.

"Yes, this is she." Her hands felt awkward holding a real phone. It'd been so long since she'd talked on anything but a cell.

"I'm Detective Sloan. I need you to come down to the station. Purely procedural. Just need you to give us an official statement."

Elise could hardly believe what she'd just heard. "What?" She pressed the phone more firmly to her ear as if that would change the Detective's words. A statement? For finding a dead body?

"We may need to fingerprint you. There is another set, not yet identified—that's all over that room."

"If they're mine, that wouldn't be weird. I was just up there the other day!" Elise stammered. She immediately became on guard at his accusation.

"Miss Pepper," his voice was a low hiss like a cat after a mouse. "What were you up there for?"

"Dave…"

The Detective made a noise that she mentioned the store owner by his first name.

She continued boldly. "Dave, my boss, took me through it." At the second mention of his name, the bookstore owner looked up. He did not appear happy.

"So you're quite comfortable with the layout of the room then, I'm assuming?"

She could hear scratching as if Detective Sloan were jotting on paper. Elise wanted to reach through the phone and grab him by the lapel and give him a good shake. Why was he turning her words around like it was a guilty statement?

"I wasn't exactly comfortable. We were trying to figure out the puzzles." She breathed out slowly.

"Puzzles, huh?" Detective Sloan gave a short chuckle. "You good at puzzles?"

"What do you mean?" Every sense in Elise rang its alarm. This guy was out for something.

"It's in my notes you went upstairs by a hidden door."

"I told them yesterday, I had to get upstairs. The men were stuck in the room."

"All of them trapped in a way that led to a man's death."

She turned around to face the window and stuck her chin up. *I will not let him intimidate me.* "I'm sorry he died but I had nothing to do with it. It's ridiculous to even think I did."

"Did I say that you did?"

"Your line of questioning sounds accusative."

He continued as if she'd said nothing. "You were the first one in there."

"I was not. His friends were there with him."

There was a long pause on the other end before he let out a slow breath. "You must think we're stupid."

"The level of your intellect is none of my business," Elise snapped back. "But it does come into question when you seem to believe a woman of my size could kill a two-hundred-and-fifty-pound man."

She heard him scribble some more. *Why would he write that down?*

"You seem familiar with his weight then," he said when he finished scribbling.

Elise felt heat as her face flushed. "What are you talking about? It's just a guess based on his size. I did see him, you know."

"I'm sure you have. You may actually know him better than you're letting on." He breathed heavily, letting that sink in. "Why don't you come down now so we can continue this in person?"

"Shouldn't I be calling my lawyer?"

"Miss Pepper," The Detective's voice was immediately softer. "I can see how this is coming across, but I promise you, this is just routine questioning. I'll be bringing everyone down that was at the bookstore that day."

Elise closed her eyes feeling a weight descend on her. "Fine. I'll be right there," she muttered before handing the phone back to Dave. Her boss nodded goodbye to her as he finished the conversation with Detective Sloan.

Like I said, I have to do everything twice today. With her phone to her ear, Elise got back in her car. When Brad didn't answer, she sighed and drove to the station.

The police station was fairly empty, with just two cars parked in the lot. Inside, the city clerk pointed down a hallway when Elise asked where Detective Sloan's office was. "First door on the left!" she called after Elise.

Elise marched her way down the hall and found the door. She sniffed the air, and fought to keep from wrinkling her nose. Coffee, she decided, did not always smell good. Not when it's stale. And bitter. And left in a pot to overheat for hours on end. Straightening her shoulders, she knocked on the door.

"Come in," rang out the same authoritarian voice she'd just heard through the phone.

Elise adjusted her face into an emotionless mask and walked in.

"Miss Pepper," Detective Sloan said by way of greeting. He pointed with a pencil to a chair in front of the desk and pulled a pad of paper closer to him. *Like I figured.*

"Detective." She sat in the chair and primly straightened her back.

"As I was saying on the phone, I'm wondering how well you knew the victim, Steve Miller."

"I'd never seen him before yesterday."

"No? Never?" He smiled. His grin looked lopsided as his lip hung up on a crooked canine tooth.

Elise stared at him and waited. It didn't seem to do any good to try to defend herself. She'd let him lead the conversation instead of making her feel like she was digging herself in deeper. He had to be bluffing. What could he possibly have on her?

"Miss Pepper, I wish you'd work with me here. Woman-up and admit what really took place. You come clean and we can help you. I know you didn't really want this to happen."

The sudden softness in the Detective's voice almost brought tears to her eyes. For a moment, after feeling alienated and accused, it made her think he was finally in her corner.

Stop. This is a trick.

"If you really want to help me, you can tell me why I'm here." Elise crossed her arms before her. She wasn't going to fall for his mind trick.

His face hardened and he tapped his notebook like the evidence was right there. "We know you needed money."

"What do you mean?"

"The money that'll come from the sale of the stolen book. Come on. Don't act like we're stupid."

The detective passed over a piece of paper on the table. She glanced at and sucked in her breath.

It was the same picture stuck under her wiper a few nights before.

"How did you get this?" She suddenly felt weak.

"Just tell me who's working with you. Where's the book?"

She glanced at the clock on the wall. It was broken, with the second hand bouncing back and forth in place. "I don't know what you're talking about. I just work at the bookstore as the cashier, and sometimes make an espresso if I'm lucky. I would never steal the book and it makes no sense that I would kill the banker. I don't even know how he died."

"I already told you that we've found extra fingerprints."

Elise fought the urge to wipe the tips of her fingers against her pants. She balled her hand into a fist instead. The Detective's eyebrows flickered at the movement and he made another note.

"And I already explained to you why my fingerprints could be there. I was in the room the day before as the first test subject.

"Even on the murder weapon?"

Elise felt sweat trickle down her spine. She swallowed even as the room seem to sway around her. "I think I need a lawyer."

He pushed back like a cat that had finally caught the mouse. "An attorney now? Why? We're just having a friendly little chat."

"What was the murder weapon?" Elise asked.

Detective Sloan stood and walked to the door. "Oh, aren't you clever. Playing coy? I think you know exactly what it was." He looked back, his face was insufferable.

Elise tried to hold back the sarcasm in her retort but the bite was still there. "If I knew, I wouldn't have asked."

His hands jammed into his pockets as he rocked back on his heels. "What else does a sweet little barista like you serve at the coffee stand? Cookies?"

Cookies? Dumbfounded, her mouth dropped open as she tried to come up with a response. "He choked on a cookie?"

"Choked on the poison, anyway. Now, don't you be leaving town. We'll be talking again real soon." His lips stretched into a raptor-like grin again. "Let's get your fingerprints done."

Elise's hands felt clammy at the thought. *What is going on here? What have I gotten myself into?*

She desperately wished Brad was there, but she'd probably be a sobbing mess burrowing in his arms.

Instead, she needed to be tough, and she needed a lawyer. And, only one person came to mind.

Her ex-husband, Mark.

Chapter Seven

It was nearly five o'clock that evening when the fingerprinting was finished and she was allowed to leave the police station. The whole experience was humiliating and she'd fought to keep the stiff upper lip. She was not going to let the detective see her struggling with any of this.

She dialed Mark as soon as she walked out the door. He was a big time lawyer in New York. It's not who she wanted to call—that was Brad—but she was still afraid that if she even heard Brad's voice right now she'd break down and not be able to stop.

"Long time no hear," Mark answered on the third ring. "You need bail money?" He laughed at his own joke, having always teased her about what a goody-two-shoes she was.

"I hope not, but it may be close."

At her tone, his laugh cut off. Quickly, she filled him in on what had happened in the last two days.

"Honestly, it sounds like they just want to scare you. If they really had something they wouldn't be calling, they'd be knocking on your door. Just don't sign anything, and if they tell you to come down again, call me first."

"Thanks, Mark." Elise said, relief making her voice higher than natural.

"Hey, I wasn't always a bad guy."

"Mmm. How's Jennifer?" The corner of her mouth raised in a half-smile. It had been long enough that his affair didn't hurt anymore.

"All right, all right," he grumped back. She could picture him rolling his eyes the way he always had when she provoked him.

"I'm just kidding, Mark. I hope things are well. I want you to be happy."

"You too, sweetheart. You know I'll always love you." He cleared his throat and continued light-heartedly, "Those bad guys bug you again, let me know. I won't let them bring you down. But don't worry, they're just fishing right now."

Feeling a bit more secure, she ended the call. She zipped a text off to Brad, then headed back to the store.

Dave looked up from his book when she came in. "Everything okay?" His voice sounded tight with concern.

"Yep," Elise slung her purse off her shoulder and onto the counter. She rubbed her temple and gave him a smile. "They just wanted an official account of my story."

He got up and poured her a mug of coffee. "It's definitely been exciting around here lately."

She eyed him to see if it was a dig at her recent hiring, but he had settled back on his stool with an air of heaviness.

Then she remembered…his family heirloom had been stolen.

"Dave, I'm so sorry about the book."

"Yeah. Just sucks. They took my laptop to examine the video." He leaned on the stool and Elise could see he was struggling to keep his emotions at bay. "I have to admit, I already watched it. All that it shows is a hand, and then the screen blanks out."

"Why did it blank out?"

He raised his finger to point. "Someone covered the lens with black spray paint. And whoever it was knew exactly where the camera was located."

"Can you hear anything?"

Slowly, he shook his head. "There's no sound, just video."

"The police will find it. It will pop up somewhere when they try to sell it."

He sarcastically snorted. "You realize that relics are sold all the time underground. Some of the world's most famous ancient paintings and sculptures are missing, squirreled away in someone's house." He sighed again. "Anyway, if you think you've got this, I'm going to head home."

"Going to write?"

He half-heartedly shrugged. "Or nap."

"Aw." Elise frowned. There was nothing she could do to make it better. "Hang in there. Have hope yet."

"Yeah, yeah," he said, scooping his jacket from the hook on the back wall of the coffee stand. "What will be, will be, I guess." He slumped to the door. The chime of the bell didn't ring like it normally did when he closed it slowly behind him.

Elise glanced around the store. The glass case where the book had been was cleaned up, leaving the stand bare and forlorn. Her skin prickled a little as the quietness of the room became almost an oppression.

Normally, she loved working alone—the smell of the coffee mixed with the books and cinnamon diffuser that Dave had installed. She could read to her heart's content.

But she was the main suspect of a murdered man— here in this very building—coupled with the picture of her and threatening note made being alone the last thing she wanted.

Brad had promised via a text to drop by the store later, which helped. She dialed Lavina, knowing Dave would understand her talking on company time.

"Are you okay?" The first words out of Lavina's mouth came in a rush.

"Well, hello to you too!" Elise smiled at her friend's voice.

"You aren't texting me so there has to be an emergency," Lavina quipped back. "I swear, I'm about to start a GoFundMe to get you a security guard. My heart can't take this!"

"I should have texted, but I got lonely."

"Where are you? At work?"

"Yes, and it's especially spooky today." Elise shivered and pulled her cardigan closer.

"You want me to come down there?" Lavina's concern laced through her voice. "I have an event at the Children's Hospital in a little bit, but I can drop in early if you need me."

More than anything, Elise wanted her friend there. But she was a big girl. She could do this on her own. "No, it's okay. Have fun."

Just then, her phone vibrated with an incoming text. It was from Brad. She read the text- **Forensic confirms it's your fingerprints. Don't worry. You already knew that would be the case. I've got your back and we'll get through this.**

Elise knew that as a police officer, Brad was keeping quiet tabs on the case at the station. But he could only fill her in and not do much else. She appreciated the heads up, but at the same time, her eyes closed as a feeling of desperation gripped her. *How could this be happening? They're going to send me to jail for this!*

No. I'm not going to let that happen. There has to be something more that they missed.

She knew what she was going to do next, even though she hadn't let the thought completely form in her head. With a deep breath, Elise walked across the room. She gripped the handrail and looked up the stairs with trepidation.

Yellow tape, like a limbo bar, was strung across the top of the stairwell. Its end trailed down the wooden treads like a child's forgotten slinky.

Taking a deep breath, she walked up the stairs, unable to help the wince as her shoes clattered on the lacquered steps.

I'll be super careful not to disturb anything, but I have to see for myself.

The doorknob twisted under her hand and the door opened, unlike last time. The inky black of the room seemed to reach out and try to suck her in. Chills trickled down her spine as if the man's ghost were in the room taunting her to come in deeper. *Come in, come right in....*

Stop it! She scolded herself and rubbed her arms briskly to smooth away the goosebumps. Without waiting for her eyes to adjust anymore, she walked in. Sometimes you have to show your imagination who's boss.

A long squeak behind her made her spin around. The door slowly began to close. Frantically, she sprang for the entry way, her fingers catching the door just before it met the frame. She swallowed hard, remembering how the door would lock from this side, leaving no way out but through the escape room.

The pitch-black escape room.

Elise untied her shoe and propped it under the door. Satisfied it was secure, she flipped on the flashlight app on her cell phone. What was she looking for? She had no idea. But there might be something.

She flashed the light around, taking in the game, the pipes, and wires. There was the Cheshire cat smiling from its lounging place amongst a tree of branching pipes. His swirling eyes creeped her out. There was the dancing teapot, the tipped hat on top of a corkscrewed-eyed rabbit, a hookah pipe, and a many-shoed caterpillar.

The light danced off the table that once held the plate of cookies. The cookies were long gone, having been taken into evidence. Elise shivered to think she'd nearly eaten from that plate. She flipped the beam up to the ceiling and traced from corner to corner. Then, crouching down to her knees, she did the same to the floor.

Something glittered white under the peg machine.

She glanced at the door to be sure it would stay wedged open and then climbed down to her belly. Stretching her arm as far as she could, she reached under the contraption for it. About four inches long, her fingertips brushed against it and pushed it along. With a grunt, she stretched more, her toes pushing for purchase against the floor.

Just about had it. Almost there.

It moved out of reach again.

She released the breath she hadn't realized she'd been holding and pushed back into a sitting position. Flashing the light, she searched around the room for anything that could help.

The ladle came into view, the same one she'd used to fill the vase with water to retrieve the key. She snatched it up and returned to the cabinet.

With her cell angled just right, she spotted the object again. Her tongue wet her lips. One more push and it could disappear behind the leg of the cabinet. She had to hook it carefully with the ladle.

Carefully, she weaved the utensil under the carved embellishment of the trim. She pushed it along the floor, stopping just before the white glittering item.

She had one chance.

Her fingers trembled from the effort of moving slowly and carefully. This was like a game of Operation like she'd never played before. Her muscles tensed and the scoop of the ladle rose and rested on the item, pushing it another centimeter away. She'd never been very good at that stupid game.

She got a finger around the handle and lifted the scoop part again. This time she was able to get it on the other side of the item. Slowly, she pulled the ladle towards her, dragging the item closer.

Muscle fatigue caused her arm to shake, and her shoulder ached from being held at a weird angle. But the item was nearly within reach.

Finally, she could grab it with her fingers and drew it out. It was smooth and carved at the same time. She held it under the light of her cell.

A glass pipe. Where did this come from? She turned it over in her hands. Might it have DNA on it?

Her eyelids fluttered close.

Probably.

Hers.

Brad was going to kill her.

Chapter Eight

Elise was exhausted when she got home from work that night. She opened her front door only to have it rebound off something on the other side. Frowning, she shoved at the door, feeling a bit sick as flashbacks of Steve's body blazed through her mind. She shoved harder as she saw it still wasn't opening. After a bit of effort, she finally created enough room to squeeze through. Her face flushed with frustration as she slammed the door closed and investigated what was on the other side.

Shoes.

Four pairs to be exact. Pink, white, yellow. All different styles of sneakers except for a set of ballet flats. All in a size four.

"Lucy!" Elise yelled as she reached back to lock the door.

No answer.

Elise shrugged off her purse and chucked it on the end table, then walked down the hall to the guest bedroom. The door was shut. She lightly tapped on it. "Lucy?" she called again.

From inside the room came the sounds of scuffling followed by a loud thump. A second later, the door was flung open to reveal a fifteen-year-old in a worn t-shirt and frayed jeans. The teen's brown hair was pulled back into two slightly disheveled braids. "Hi, Elise!"

Elise couldn't help but smile. Gone was the sharp, bony cheek and jaw line that the teen first had when Elise met her living out on the streets. Lucy's cheeks now were filled out like two pink apples. But, her hazel eyes still held a wariness that belied her innocent smile.

Elise took a deep breath to temper her next words. "So, did you have a good day at a school?"

"Turned in my homework and got a B on my Chemistry test. Oh, yeah! I finished in third place in practice today." The teen flushed with apparent pride as she hung onto the door, swinging it slightly.

"You had track today? I didn't know that."

"Yep. And then I walked those dogs for you. Frodo and Winnie are such stinkers. They actually tied their leashes into a knot trying to chase after a squirrel!"

Elise laughed. She was grateful that Lucy had taken over her dog walking business. It was good for Mrs. Perkins and Mrs. Campbell, too. The two elderly women doted on Lucy and always had snacks and a listening ear waiting for her when she stopped by.

"So, listen," Elise began cautiously. "About those shoes at the front door, they all ganged up on me and tried to keep me locked outside."

"Outside?"

"Yeah. They jammed the door shut. I could barely open it."

Lucy's cheeks went even pinker. "Oh, my gosh! I'm sorry! I'll go get them right now." The teen rushed out of the room for the shoes.

"No worries," Elise called after her. "But maybe we can keep the shoe gang secluded to your closet for the future."

"You got it." Lucy returned with her arms full of sneakers. She chucked them into her room.

Elise snorted. Teenagers. "Thanks. Now, how about some dinner?" She walked into the kitchen.

"I'm pretty full. Mrs. Perkins fed me some Salisbury steak." Lucy answered with a contented sigh.

Elise's stomach growled at the thought of the homemade meal. Gravy over mashed potatoes and seasoned meat. *Mmm.* She nearly whimpered as she opened the cupboard to look for a cup-of-soup.

"Oh, by the way. She sent a plate home for you, too!" Lucy announced as she followed her. The teen opened the fridge and pulled out a tin-foil-covered plate. Elise took it from her with a heart warm from gratitude. Her smile grew even bigger as she peeled back the tinfoil. Two beef patties and a big mound of gravy-covered mashed potatoes. Enough for Brad.

Without further delay, she got a couple of plates from the cupboard and divided the food. She licked her fingers and put her plate into the microwave.

"Here's the mail," Lucy said from where she perched on a bar stool. She swiveled the stool back and forth. "The mailman comes late around here."

"Late?" Elise said, her brows furrowing. That was unusual. Usually the mailman arrived early in the morning.

"Yeah. And he was driving a brown truck."

Elise looked at her, startled. "Huh. That's weird. Maybe he was a new guy?" She reached for the stack of letters on the counter and shuffled through them. Bill. Bill. An ad for an oil change.

Wait. What's this?

Her address was typed across the envelope, not unusual. But what had caught her eye was that the return address consisted of a hand-drawn rabbit.

"I noticed that, too," Lucy remarked as Elise ran her thumb over the drawing. "It's pretty cool! Maybe something to do with the fair?"

"Maybe." Elise started to open the envelope when the microwave dinged. Her stomach growled again, commanding her attention with all the elegance of a bull in a china shop.

74

The gravy and potatoes melted in her mouth at the first bite. Her eyes automatically closed as she took a moment to savor the home-cooked food. What was it about someone else's cooking that tasted so much better? She didn't know and didn't care as she cut into the meat. Perfection.

"You really were hungry, huh?" Lucy watched her, one thin eyebrow raised in question.

"I forgot to bring my lunch today. And it was a pretty crappy day." Then, fork poised, she turned her attention back to the envelope.

"Okay, let's see what this says." She took another quick bite before opening it up.

Inside was a simple folded piece of paper. She flattened it out to reveal another drawing across the top. This one was of a little girl in an iconic apron looking wide-eyed at a caterpillar curled up on a mushroom. Flowers with smiling faces trailed down both sides of the paper. The bottom of the paper was marred by a black hole. On either side of the hole were two more flowers.

But these flowers were not so pleasant. Instead of smiles, their mouths were open to reveal sharp teeth. Tendrils rose from the flowers and snaked up the page to secure around the little girl's ankle.

Words written in calligraphy danced in between the vines.

Tic-Toc the clock's about to stop.

What if Alice never returned from the rabbit hole?

Would she, could she have married?

The hare may be calling her back.

Underneath the words were four hearts.

Elise swallowed hard and looked at Lucy. The teen had just put a piece of gum in her mouth and was snapping a bubble.

"What?" she asked at Elise's expression. "Is it a bill after all?"

"I think it's something worse." Elise laid the letter down and unconsciously wiped her fingers on the side of her pants with a shudder. "Much worse."

Chapter Nine

The next morning, Elise watched a laughing troop of teens ascend the stairs for the Escape Room. They'd heard about the murder on social media and obviously were thrill seekers. A shiver ran lightly down her arms and she reached for her sweater. *How could Jake and Thomas just open back up for business like nothing ever happened?*

She glanced at the clock and noted the time. The teens would be back down in a little over an hour.

Another tremor shook her. A lot can happen in an hour.

In fact, just two hours before, the construction workers had been working in the room, which had been cleared earlier from the investigation.

She frowned as she remembered one of the contractors, a short man with curly hair, who'd winked at her every time he passed. One or two winks, fine, but he'd come up and down the stairs winking like his eye had a tic. It even bugged his co-worker, Harry, who finally shoved him in the shoulder to get him to quit, yelling, "Knock it off, you little maggot."

The bell above the door rang and Lavina breezed in, looking like an actress walking straight off of the set in her fitted dress and rhinestone sunglasses. She carried a bag over her arm, along with a giant, yellow purse.

"Darlin'!" she trilled, crossing over the wood floor with mincing steps.

"Hi, Vi," Elise said. "You here for some coffee?" She smirked, knowing how Lavina liked her sweet tea. And her Manhattans.

"Oh, aren't you just the cutest thing," Lavina drolled. She lifted her glasses and set them on top of her head. "No, I'm here to show you my latest and greatest." She set the purse on the counter and looked at Elise expectantly. A small frown appeared at Elise's lack of reaction. For good measure, Vi turned the purse slightly. "No?" Lavina said. "You aren't going to say anything?"

"Say anything?" Elise glanced at the purse. "Is this new? Lovely color."

"Darlin', I know you are insistent about embracing a bohemian fashion sense, but surely…" she looked at Elise in astonishment. "Surely you realize this *is* a Birkin?"

"Oh…." Elise tried hard to look suitably impressed.

Lavina narrowed her eyes, not buying it.

Elise gave it a second attempt. "Wow! A Birkin?"

A long sigh issued from Lavina. "What am I going to do with you?" She glanced at Elise. "Don't answer that. At any rate, my honeybear Mr. G decided to surprise me.

And now, tonight, I'm going to surprise him." She gave a lascivious wink.

Elise shook her head. "Too much info, Vi. What've I told you about that?"

Lavina laughed. "You know how I like to tease you. At any rate, since I was the recipient of such generosity, I wanted to pass it on. If anyone deserves a prize after the other day, it's you. Here." She set the bag on the counter.

Elise opened it and pulled out a cerulean-blue silk scarf. Her mouth dropped open. "Wow! It's gorgeous!"

Lavina preened. "It's Hermes. We picked it up at the same time. Put it on!"

"Okay…." Elise felt a twinge of awkwardness as she tried to wind the scarf around her throat. *Something like this.* She wound it around again.

Lavina watched with a look akin to horror. Her hands fidgeted as she gave Elise a stiff smile. Finally, it seemed she couldn't stand it any longer.

"Here! Give me that." Lavina disentangled the scarf and soon had it draped around Elise's neck. "Much better." She smiled with satisfaction. The smile quickly dropped as she glanced at Elise's T-shirt. "Well, it seems to prove a scarf truly can dress anything up."

"Do I look okay?" Elise asked.

Lavina's smile was back at full wattage. "Stunning." She picked up her purse. "Now, I'm off to lunch. I just wanted to peek in on you and make sure you were okay after that dreadful nonsense the other day."

Elise cringed. Only Vi would word it that way.

Lavina waggled her fingers in goodbye and daintily stepped to the door. "See you soon!" she promised as she left the store.

Elise smiled and touched the scarf. Good friends were like gold, and she couldn't imagine her life without Lavina.

Because right about now, she needed all the support she could get. Sighing, she wiped the counter with the towel and picked up a few scattered sugar packages. She hadn't heard back from the detective, but that didn't mean he wasn't planning on dropping in on her later like a bomb.

Her life as she knew it, suddenly felt very fragile. The struggles and stresses that she'd faced in the past seemed minuscule in comparison to being investigated for a murder.

But, like Brad had tried to remind her the night before, they hadn't arrested her. That meant they didn't have enough evidence.

Yet.

All right, Elise. Focus. You can't always go to worse case scenario. When has that ever helped, anyway?

Brad had been much more concerned about the letter and took it with him to the station today. Lucy described the truck that she'd assumed had been the mailman, and Brad was doing an off-the-clock investigation on who it could be.

Something was stuck to the counter and she tried to scrape it with a fingernail.

"What are you looking at?" A male voice caused her to jump.

It was the tall construction worker, Harry.

"Whoa, sorry to scare you." He put his hands up in the air. "I thought I'd grab a coffee before I left."

"Sorry, I was concentrating on getting that off."

He scraped at it with his thumb. "Looks like that Liquid Weld stuff."

"Oh, yeah?" she said rinsing her hands. "What's that?"

"A type of glue—really, really strong stuff." He continued to pick at it before giving up.

"So, what can I get you?" she asked, drying her hands.

He frowned as he studied the menu on the wall. "You have something that isn't all fru-fru?"

Elise bit her lip to keep from laughing. She hardly dared repeat his word in case the giggle escaped. "You mean you want a plain coffee?"

"Yeah. They serve that here?"

"Of course. It *is* a coffee shop."

His eyes twinkled as they caught hers. "Go ahead and laugh. I can see it on your face." He settled onto one of the barstools and pulled out a plastic-wrapped cookie from the basket. He turned the cookie over in his hands.

"I'm not laughing," Elise said, with a grin. "Now, what size do you want?"

"I don't know. About this big?" He demonstrated with his hands.

Good grief. Had this guy ever ordered a coffee before? "A large then. Okay," Her gaze flickered to the basket. "You want a cookie too?"

"Nah. I was just curious." His mouth curved into a half-grin. "Is this the type of cookie that killed the dude?" He returned it to the basket.

Elise almost dropped the coffee cup. She straightened her shoulders and finished filling the cup from the carafe. "How did you hear that?" she asked calmly as she grabbed a lid. "You want room for cream?"

His eyebrows quirked in confusion.

"Would you like it filled to the brim or have me leave some room for cream."

"Ah, no. Black is fine." His good-natured grin was back. "Dave told me this morning. He said the cops took the entire batch from yesterday so he had to pick up new ones for today."

"That's just creepy," she said as she pushed the plastic lid on the cup and slid it toward him. "You guys are still working up there? I thought the construction was done."

"Jake and Thomas had me and Hamish doing some last minute repairs."

"Hamish?" Elise tried to get an image of a cartoon pig out of her mind.

Harry laughed. "I know. It's a weird name, huh? He's a good guy. Anyway, the cops really did a number on the Escape Room when they were shaking it down for evidence."

"Makes sense." Elise nodded. *But I'm the one that found the pipe. I wonder if they're considering Thomas and Jake as suspects too?*

"Well, nice chatting with you." Harry pushed over a five dollar bill and lifted the cup as a way of saying goodbye.

"Have a good day." Elise smiled, collecting the money.

A startled squeal and loud laughter came from the room upstairs. Elise could imagine the young teen girls grabbing on to their date's arms as they navigated through the dark room. She could picture what they were seeing—the flashing neon signs, the puzzle leading to the key for the next room, the clock.

I wonder what puzzle they used to replace the cookie one?

Thinking about the cookie stressed her out. She couldn't help replaying that day again, and her mouth went dry as the seconds ticked by. Glancing down, she realized she'd grabbed the towel and been wiping the spot with the weld glue over and over. Anxiously, she looked at the clock.

Dear Lord, this was about the time when the man screamed....

Her skin prickled at the memory.

Cleaning wasn't working to calm her down like she'd hoped. She closed her eyes and took a couple breaths, trying to picture a beach. Ocean waves. Instead, more memories flashed from that day. She pulled a glass from the cupboard and filled it with water from the faucet. Gulping it down, she tried to steady herself.

It's fine. I'm fine. With a deep breath, she rinsed the glass and opened the dishwasher. Her muscles slowly began to unclench. *I've got this.*

A scream ripped through the air.

Chapter Ten

The glass slipped from Elise's fingers and smashed unnoticed on the floor. Her gaze locked on the door to the upper room.

No! Not again!

She looked at the back stairwell and hesitated. If she went up those stairs again would it just be used against her?

"Help! Help!" A woman screams pierced the air.

Run.

Elise sprinted through the broom closet and up the back steps. She yanked on the door.

It was stuck. Someone pounded on the other side and clung to the doorknob, making it immovable.

"Let go so I can open it!" Elise screamed. The doorknob turned then and she wrenched it open. A girl tumbled into her arms and nearly knocked her back down the stairs.

"What's the matter? What's going on?" Elise pushed the trembling girl away by the shoulders and searched her eyes. "Is someone hurt?" Her heart pounded.

"Hurt?" The girl's blue eyes were huge and tear-filled as she stared blankly up at her.

Elise looked back into the dark room. The picture had been torn off the wall and lay on the floor. "Who's hurt? What happened?"

Laughter carried over from the other side of the room. "Jules? You scared?"

The young woman's body still trembled but she managed a smile. "I'm not too good in dark places like these, I guess."

Just then, Thomas came tearing up the stairs with a look of terror pasted to his face. "What happened?" he asked Elise. The young man's head swiveled as he looked from teen to teen.

The group of kids filled him in on the girl's fear of the dark. Thomas grabbed his chest and staggered back relieved. "You guys nearly killed me!"

Elise gave him a brittle smile and the two of them headed down the stairs, leaving the group of teens upstairs to continue to figure out the game. The young woman settled on the top step to wait for her friends.

Once out of sight, Elise turned with anger to Thomas. "You think you're scared, now? I'm about to kill you, having had to go through this *twice* now. You absolutely have to find a better way to monitor this than through your computer at a restaurant."

"Yeah, I know." He looked glumly at the room. "This place is going to be the death of me."

"I hope not literally." Elise snapped back.

Thomas looked sick at her words.

"Bad choice of words, there," he admitted. "Sorry about that. I promise we'll figure out a better way. Maybe even hang out in this coffee area, here." He glanced at her. "So, uh, by the way, how are things going?"

"Going?" Elise was still fuming as she walked back to the coffee counter and picked up the broken glass on the ground.

"Yeah," Thomas cracked his knuckles, his hands appearing overly-large at the end of his gangly arms. He cleared his throat as if uncomfortable. "With, uh, the investigation."

Elise shrugged. "I guess I'm still their only lead. I haven't heard different. It's pretty crazy."

"I mean, how can they think that?" He shrugged and gave a nervous laugh. "They must be desperate to really think you did it."

"I guess so." Elise sighed and rolled her shoulders. She felt the tension in her muscles start to dissipate.

"Did they ever say why they think you did it?" He rubbed the back of his neck. "That sounds weird even to ask."

Elise didn't want to get into the extortion aspect of the photo and just kept it simple. "They think I swiped the book, *Alice in Wonderland*."

Thomas stared at the wood floors with a frown.

Elise knew that feeling, the one where you didn't know what to say or how to get out of a conversation, and gave him a way out. "So, how did you get here so fast?" With a glare, she added, "Although not fast enough."

He flushed so she smiled to let him know this time she was kidding.

"We were watching from the restaurant," Thomas said. "Just a lot closer this time. I've got that camera in there so we can monitor it."

"That's right!" Elise paused as her memory chimed. "Weren't you saying something about that the other day?" She felt a zing of hope. "Wasn't the camera operating on the day of the murder?"

He swallowed, clearly uncomfortable with the word *murder* in association to his room, and nodded.

"But, I think you said that it blacked out?" Elise pressed. "Did you ever watch the entire thing?" The excitement began to build, making her nearly jump up and down. She was half tempted to grab him by the arms and shake him. *Chill. You are a grown up here.*

Thomas said. "No, we didn't bother after the picture cut out."

"So, you never showed it to the police?"

"I didn't think it would be helpful without a picture."

"I know this is a long shot, but do you think we could just try and look at it one more time?"

"Yeah, why not. I owe you after today." Thomas grabbed his phone and typed. "Ok, there. Sent a text to Jake to bring the laptop here."

The buzzer sounded upstairs, making Elise jump. Thomas glanced at his cell again. "No worries. That's just the timer's saying the kids didn't solve the room in an hour."

Moments later, the group of teens pounded down the stairs and headed, laughing, out the door. On their way, they passed Jake who was walking in.

"What's up?" Jake asked Thomas. He had the laptop firmly under his other arm.

"Elise was wondering if she could check out the footage from the room. From, you know, the other day."

"D-day, the only day you could mean." Jake set the laptop on the counter with a clatter. He opened it and began typing. "Let's try it. Not sure how far back this is going to go, though." Then, glancing up, he asked, "Did you tell her about the problem?"

"Yeah," Thomas turned to Elise. "We figured out why the picture disappeared. The camera inside the room was vandalized." He started to crack his knuckles again and ended up jamming his hands into his pockets.

Elise had a feeling she knew what it was. "Black paint?"

Thomas nodded.

"Just like what happened to Dave's," Elise concluded with a sigh.

Jake typed a few more commands until the screen came up, and then clicked an arrow to run back the recording. It was a slow process and Elise thought she would scream as anxiety built inside of her.

Finally, he grinned. "Okay, then. Here we go." His face shone with youthful enthusiasm as he shoved the screen towards her.

She watched herself—face tight in fear—bang on the escape room's door at the top of the stairs. Elise hadn't realized there had been a camera mounted to the door frame. Seconds later, she disappeared from the screen as she ran back down the stairs. She reappeared on another screen at the back door. The other screen was dark.

"Can you rewind it a little further?" she asked.

He tried with one more swipe and then frowned. "It won't go back anymore."

She leaned over and rewound it again. Something had caught her attention from the first scene. *What was that?* A smudge moved in one of the corners of the screen.

"Can you zoom in right there?" She pointed.

Jake frowned and typed furiously on the screen. The screen enlarged but the resolution blurred. He rewound it again.

They all watched carefully. Elise found herself holding her breath.

"It's a hat," Thomas finally muttered.

Elise felt a thrill of excitement. True, the hat showed on the screen for just a moment, but it was proof she wasn't the only one in the store that day. She swiped to rewind it again. *Ahh. So frustrating.* If only she could go back just a few more seconds, she'd be able to see who it was.

"We have to show this to the cops," she said, feeling hope for the first time.

Thomas nodded and took a screen shot of it. "You weren't alone that day, Elise. Someone was in here with you."

She shivered, realizing she hadn't had a clue.

Chapter Eleven

After work that evening, Elise took a moment of quiet out on her front stoop with her mug of coffee, soaking in the late afternoon sunshine as it hit her face. *I swear life can be broken down to simple pleasures like this. You get enough of them beaded together as life's experiences and you can die a rich man.*

Or woman. She snorted and took another sip. *Almost had a good analogy there.*

Just before her shift had ended, Jake and Thomas had met with Detective Sloan. The detective hadn't seemed pleased with the new evidence. He'd subtly insinuated that Jake had held on to the recording for some reason, leaving both Jake and Thomas shaken after the interview. Elise had felt slightly relieved at the thought that maybe the detective treated all of his interviews that way, and she wasn't alone.

So, all in all, it was good news for Elise. The video proved that she hadn't been alone that day when the bankers had entered the Escape Room. There was now another suspect.

A loud bang came from the new neighbor's house, grabbing her attention. A man had climbed out of a truck and slammed the driver's door. Across the side of the white truck was a cartoon hammer and handsaw, hemmed in by the words, "Doorknob Home Repairs."

The coverall-covered man hurried up to the front door and knocked boldly. It was the young wife who answered. Elise sipped from her mug and watched as the wife reached out and touched the door frame — or was it the worker's sleeve? — before she stepped back to let him in the house.

Interesting. Elise studied the truck again. The bed was filled with boards along with a metal rack structure that held different sizes of pipe.

A plumber? Electrician? What exactly does 'Home Repairs' entail?

This reminded Elise of the state of disrepair her own front porch had fallen into. She picked at a piece of peeling paint on the step next to her, frowning as the paint peeled back into a long strip. *How do I even fix this? Sand it?* Her gaze traveled up the front of the house, spotting more peeling spots on the walls. A depressed groan eased out of her. *Sand the whole house?*

Not going to think about that right now. She stood and set the mug on the railing. Then she stepped down the stairs and examined the front flower beds.

The flowers appeared as if they felt a bit reproachful towards her, surrounded as they were by weeds. They lifted choked-out leaves to the sun.

"I'm sorry. I'm sorry," Elise muttered, dropping to her knees. She dug into the dirt and twisted the weed stems, yanking the weeds out with a hard pull.

After a little bit, the bed already seemed better, with a pile of wilting weeds drying in the driveway. Elise heard another slam and looked up just in time to see the home repair truck speed away. A twenty minute home repair? Her brow furrowed as she went back to pulling weeds. She carefully shook the dirt out of the last clump roots before tossing the plant.

Another vehicle pulled up across the street. *What is this, musical cars?* She couldn't help looking again, keenly aware she was only one small step from becoming that nosy neighbor from the movie *That Darn Cat.*

It was Seth. He shut the car door and glanced around. Catching her eye, he lifted his hand in greeting.

What's this? Oh great, he's coming over. Elise felt her cheeks heat at being caught snooping on him. She cleared her throat and pushed her hair off her face as she stood up to greet him.

"Hi, Seth," she said quietly.

"Hey! How are you?" His dimples creased with his easy smile. He reminded her of the bankers earlier, dressed as he was in a dark blue business suit with the jacket hanging open. As he reached her, he stuck a finger in his tie and loosened it. "Ahh, that's better. Nothing like a banker's noose to remind me how much I like t-shirts."

Odd choice of words, given what I was just thinking. Elise gave a small chuckle. "I can imagine."

"Yeah, that's the way it goes, though. Somebody's got to bring home the bacon. Wife's kinda demanding that way." He surveyed her flower garden. "Looks great! You weeding?"

Biting back a smart-alecky reply, Elise nodded. "I figure I'd better get at it before someone complained."

"Oh," His eyebrows knotted in concern. "People complain around here?"

Elise shook her head. That darn dry humor of hers. Nobody got it. "No, I'm just kidding. But they probably should have. It was looking so shabby."

"Nah. It just looked like you've been busy is all. I just wanted to make sure so that no one got back to our landlords that we weren't taking care of the place or something." Again that boyish grin. "So, I've been meaning to ask, do you have any plans for this weekend?"

"Plans?"

"Yeah, uh, with that cop fellow?" His brow wrinkled.

"Oh, Brad? He's working."

"Aww. That's too bad. Well, we wanted to invite the two of you over. You're welcome to come alone." He dipped his head in the direction of his house where Elise eyed nervously, waiting for Linda to come out. "We're playing the Settlers of Catan. Beer, nachos that sort of thing." His brown eyes studied her for a second. One dimple formed. "I hope you can come."

The pause between them grew as Elise struggled with the correct response. "Uh, I'd love to but I need to stay home with Lucy."

"Lucy?"

"My niece." Elise didn't want to explain the relationship. In fact, she was about done with the conversation. "Which reminds me, I need to get dinner started."

He nodded before reaching out toward her face. She automatically flinched and pulled away.

"Shh. Don't move." He grabbed her shoulder to steady her and wiped at her cheek. "You had a little bit of dirt there," he said as an explanation as he released her.

Elise fought the urge to wipe her cheek. "Okay, thanks. Next time just let me know."

He laughed. "I'm sorry. It just was so cute I couldn't resist."

Okay then.

"Thank you for inviting me. Maybe next time we can make it." Elise hoped her voice sounded firm and made the point that she wouldn't come alone.

"No problem. Anyway, I guess I should get back. See what the wife's been up to all day. Probably nothing." He made a face.

Do not say anything. This isn't your circus. Just smile and go into the house.

Elise wrestled with that inner voice for a moment, wanting to tell him off for sounding so insulting. But, in reality, it was their lives and their marriage.

And, really, she didn't know what Linda did all day. Especially since the home repair guy seemed awfully friendly.

She felt proud of herself when she managed a wave and a quick return to her porch, having escaped adding any more drama.

Chapter Twelve

Elise grabbed the mug from the railing and walked into the house. *Whoa.* She looked around. It was as if a clothing bomb had gone off in the living room. *I'm not single anymore.* She gathered sweaters, a hoody, and three more pairs of shoes by the door as she tried to straighten up.

Max, her orange tabby cat, followed at her feet and meowed as if to remind her it was time for a cat treat.

"You little scamp. No more treats for you. I told you that Dr. Wendt would put you on a diet the next time you saw him, and see what happened? You're on diet cat food." She pointed to the new bag of food sitting on the kitchen counter. The bag featured a healthy cat that even seemed to smile behind perfectly groomed whiskers.

Quite unlike Max, who hated his new food. He'd been on a cat food semi-strike, ever since she'd brought it home. It nearly broke Elise's heart to see him come running with excitement when he heard the kibble hit the bowl, only to turn his nose up when he saw that it was the despised brand.

"Are you talking to yourself again?" Lucy called from her room. Elise's cheeks heated. Having Lucy living there had put her self-talk under a microscope. She'd had no idea how much she carried on a conversation with herself until the teen continued to make comments about it.

"I'm talking to Max!" Elise called back. "Now, what do you want for dinner?"

She needed to get on it because Brad would be there soon.

Probably as hungry as Max.

Elise quickly washed her hands. Then, she opened her pantry and stared inside, as if waiting for something to jump out and inspire her. Long seconds passed as her eyes scanned the shelves. Soup, half a box of cereal, peanut butter, potatoes, and mac and cheese. She was just about to shut the door—sucking in air for an exasperated sigh—when she spied a box of Bisquick.

Ah! I can do something with this. And maybe even make it look impressive. She carried the box to the counter and scoured the back for recipes. *Make it look like I've been cooking all day.*

"What's up, chicken butt?" Lucy spun around the corner. She climbed on a bar stool and tapped the counter with her palms in a rat-a-tat-tat.

"Chicken is exactly it. Chicken and dumplings. Here, you get these," Elise shoved the box toward her and pointed to the first few ingredients, "While I get going on making the dumplings."

Lucy pulled the box over. "You excited for your birthday?"

"Yes!" Elise said. "I'm taking Brad horseback riding. But don't tell him. He doesn't know yet."

"And why don't you want him to know?" Lucy gave her a knowing smile.

"Some things are better as a surprise."

"Oh, right. I know that one. Like it's better to ask forgiveness than permission sometimes."

"Yeah," Elise cast Lucy a doubtful look. She wasn't too happy that Lucy subscribed to that motto. She'd used it many times herself in high school.

The teen focused on the back of the Bisquick box. She read the list silently, her lips slowly moving, and slid off the stool. Elise felt a flicker of amusement as she walked to the freezer repeating the ingredients to remember everything on the list. That kid was so darn sweet.

"Lard is a weird name."

"What makes you say that?" Elise asked.

"It was on another recipe on the back. If you say the word enough, it doesn't make sense anymore."

"You want to hear a weird name? I just learned a new one, today. Hamish!"

Lucy laughed. "Oh, Hamish. He's a bad guy."

Elise stopped what she was doing to stare. "How on earth do you know that?"

"He's in the *Alice and Wonderland* movie. I used to watch it all the time when I was waiting for Ma to come home. He's supposed to marry Alice."

"Weird! Well, this one is the name of one of the construction guys. Why was Hamish a bad guy in the movie, anyway?" Elsie measured what she needed into a mixing bowl and stirred it together.

"He's hoity-toity and snooty and is being forced to marry Alice. He thinks he's a gift to women but she doesn't like him."

"Hmm. Well, good for her. Now, how was school today? Learn anything interesting?"

Lucy wrinkled her freckled nose. "It was all fine except for history. I hate learning all those different political systems. And Mr. Harris keeps giving us these stupid pop tests."

"That was my least favorite subject, too," Elise began scooping balls of dough. "But it's good to understand them."

"Yeah, but how do you know which one really is the best way? Each government thinks it's the one that's right."

Elise was interrupted from having to explain—much to her relief—by the ring of her cell phone. "Hold that thought," she said, raising her index finger. She ran for the living room and scrambled in her purse for the phone. Just as she got it out—as well as a pile of tissues, keys, wallet, lipgloss, and sunglasses—the call ended.

"Hm," her brows knitted together as she read the restricted number. "Wonder who that was?"

The phone rang again. Startled, she nearly dropped it, but instead, fumbled to finally turn it on.

"Hello?" She'd briefly glanced at the screen again before answering. It was from the same restricted number.

"Are you talking to yourself again?" An unfamiliar male voice asked. It was muffled just enough to remind Elise of covering the phone with a handkerchief during slumber party prank calls.

"Excuse me?" she asked.

"You little scamp. No treats for you. I told you Dr. Wendt would put you on a diet the next time you saw him, and see what happened? You're on diet cat food." The voice dropped the words in a cold monotone.

Goosebumps traveled down Elise's neck. *What in the world?* She walked over to the window and peeled the closed blinds apart to peek through. There was no one in sight. *Someone's stalking me....*

"Who are you?" she asked again. Wasn't there a way she could track this call? She tried to remember a # sequence hack that would show the number.

"Making dumplings. Learn anything interesting?"

Elise slowly turned in the living room, her eyes searching. Where was the mic? How had he heard her? Her eyes skipped across the lamp, the china cabinet, and the bookshelf, looking for anything out of the ordinary.

"You want to talk? Talk," she said in a clipped tone, not about to be intimidated. At least, not about to show it. Her legs felt like gelatin.

A slow laugh erupted through the receiver. As hard as she tried to remain strong, the sound unnerved her even more than him repeating her conversation.

It was the sound of a madman.

She couldn't take it any longer and clicked the phone off. Her hands were shaking as she stared at the cell like it was a snake that threatened to strike.

"What's the matter?" Lucy said, before mumbling, "Oh shoot, Max! Watch out!" The cat ducked from under her foot.

Elise swallowed. "Nothing. Everything is fine."

"If everything is fine then why do you like as white as a ghost?" Lucy picked up the orange cat and leaned against the back of the couch.

Thoughts spun in Elise's head like towels in a dryer. She walked over to the front door to check it was secure. "If anyone knocks, you be sure you know who they are before you let them in."

She glanced at the teen. Lucy was looking a little scared herself.

"Tell me who was on the phone?" the girl asked, hugging the cat tighter.

"It was a prank call," Elise answered, and then held a finger up to her lips in a "shh" manner. The gesture caused the teen's mouth to drop open in surprise. Lucy immediately studied the room.

"What?" Lucy mouthed, not finding anything.

Beckoning her to follow her, Elise walked into the kitchen. "Come on. We need to get this dinner finished." She fished a pad of paper out of the drawer and scrawled out—Someone's listening to us. I don't know who yet. I don't know how.

Lucy read it and covered her mouth with her hand. Her eyes were large and dark. Elise made another shushing gesture and then gave her a quick hug. She turned back to the mixture of Bisquick and tried to make her hands stop shaking.

Lucy buried her face into the cat. Shivering, she walked closer to Elise and leaned her head against her shoulder.

Elise leaned and kissed the top of the girl's head. "It'll be okay," she whispered. "I'll keep you safe."

Chapter Thirteen

Brad was hardly able to get through the door before both of the girls were on him.

"Whoa! What's the matter? What's going on?" He set his bags down and wrapped his arm around them, his eyes wide with confusion. "Who's hurt? Who do I have to kill?"

"It was a prank call..." Lucy began.

Elise babbled over the top of her. "Hi, baby. No, nothing's wrong." She held her finger to her lips. Lucy noticed and her mouth went round with a silent "Oh."

A sharp indent grew between Brad's eyebrows. "What are you playing at here, Elise? I can tell something's...." He was cut off by Lucy's waving hand furiously shushing him.

"So! For dinner! Are you hungry?" Elise talked a mile a minute, hoping to keep Brad at bay. She hurried over to the pad of paper and snatched it up. Back at Brad's side, she held it in front of his face.

He grabbed it from her hand and read it. When he looked back at her, his eyebrows had risen. Looking confused, he shook his head. Elise scanned what she'd given him—a grocery list? Gah!—and turned the pad over.

On the other side was the note she'd written to Lucy earlier. —Someone's listening.

Brad's jaw tightened as he read. He looked around the room as the pad of paper trembled from his clenched fist. Dragging his gaze away, he gave Elise a stiff smile. "So what's for dinner?"

"I'm thinking chicken?" she asked, uncertain.

"Tonight, I think I'm going to treat you ladies." He draped his arms around their shoulders and gathered them close. "Pho? Tacos?"

"Tacos!" Lucy chimed. "I'll get my coat."

"I don't care," Elise rested her forehead against his chest, suddenly feeling drained. He drew her in closer and she smiled at the sound of his heartbeat. The feeling of safety grew and she slid her arms around him. They swayed a bit from side to side. Brad tipped her chin so that she looked at him. He winked, before dropping a kiss on her lips.

"I've got this," he breathed into her ear. He raised his head to yell at Lucy, "You ready, kiddo?"

She came careening around the corner with eyeliner on. "Do I look okay? Is my makeup even?"

"Gorgeous," Elise answered with a smile. She grabbed her purse and gathered everything back inside while Brad waited by the front door. She locked the door, and they all climbed into Brad's jeep.

"Now what's going on?" he asked, looking over his shoulder as he backed out of the driveway.

"I got a phone call," Elise began, holding up a finger to stop Lucy as the teen tried to butt in. "And the voice on the other end repeated everything Lucy and I had just said. Word for word."

"Male or female?" Brad's eyes narrowed in anger.

"Male."

"Did you recognize it?"

Elise started to shake her head no, when she stopped, startled. She *had* heard that voice before. But where?

"Actually, maybe," she answered hesitantly. She bit her lip, still trying to sort it out. Different men flashed through her memory as she tried to match the voice. Finally, she shook her head. "I just can't think of who. But it did sound familiar."

Brad's face took on a grimmer look. His grip on the gear shift tightened until his knuckles appeared white under the skin. "I don't like this. That house isn't safe. We need to find someplace for you two to stay."

"Leave my house? I can't do that. There's Max for one, and you can't have pets in your apartment. Lucy has her dog walking…why don't you stay with us?" Elise asked, stroking Brad's arm. "Maybe just you being there will discourage whoever it is. Or maybe, you'll figure out who's doing this."

"I've got to find the bug," he grumbled.

"Cool!" Lucy yelled from the back seat. She bounced forward until her head was between them. "Like real spy stuff."

"Sit back, Lucy," Elise murmured. Then, turning to Brad. "That means someone would have been in my house."

"Yeah. That's right. You lose any keys? Give any out to anyone?"

"Just you and Lavina," Elise answered, biting her lip.

She thought about it. "There was a weird thing that happened."

"What?" Brad immediately grabbed on to her words.

"The day that Steve died...I remember that my hands had been covered in oil when I started my car. It might have come from my keys."

"Why would you keep something like that from me?" Brad rolled his eyes.

"I didn't know I was keeping something. I was so shocked that I'd just done CPR, and he still died...." Elise closed her eyes at the memory. "I just put it together now." She took a deep breath to ground herself, then fished her keys out to examine them. Whatever residue that had been on them was now long gone.

Brad pulled into a hardware store and parked. "First things first, new doorknobs."

Elise climbed out after him.

He strode into the store with his brow low in a determined look. "Whoever stole the book wanted to set you up, Elise. He made a cast of your house key somehow while you were all upstairs. Clay, wax, I'm not sure. But that answers the question of how he got in."

Elise followed him, feeling slimy. Someone had been in her house. That wasn't conjecture, it was a sure thing. She shivered.

Ten minutes later, they'd paid and were back outside with two new deadbolt locks. They picked up some tacos —couldn't disappoint Lucy—and scarfed them down. Then, they stopped at Brad's apartment to pick up his drill and another object, a black box that he described as an RF signal detector. After a bit more wheedling and convincing that she didn't want to leave her home, he also packed a change of clothes, agreeing to stay over.

"When we get back to the house, everyone keep the conversation light until I find the bugs. All small talk. Or just watch TV," he shot the last comment at Lucy.

"What? Do you think I'm going to say something?" The teen scowled back.

"No, he's just warning us to be on our best acting behavior," Elise said soothingly. "We don't want to tip this guy off."

"Yeah, I want the moment where I find the guy and snap those cuffs on him to be a surprise," Brad growled.

Elise's eyebrows flickered in surprise. *It sounds more like he's thinking about snapping the stalker's neck rather than cuffs on his wrists. I've never seen Brad be anything but Mr. Calm, Cool and Collected, even in the most hair-raising investigation.*

Back at the house, Brad made quick work moving through the house with the RF signal detector. After hitting a few buttons, he slowly walked through the house with the scanner ahead of him like a dousing rod.

He ran his hands behind the picture frames and lifted one off the wall with a disgusted look. Turning it over revealed a small metal button which he pried off with his thumbnail.

He rifled through the books on the shelf and opened the china cabinet. In the kitchen, he looked under the fruit bowl and under the table. He found another bug attached to the bottom of a chair.

"Is that all?" Elise asked.

Brad put his finger to his lips and took the RF detector through both of the bedrooms. He discovered one more bug in Elise's bathroom behind the trash can.

His face was harshly lined by frown lines as he gathered all three transmitters into his hand and brought them out to his jeep. Then he set to work changing out the locks. Twenty minutes later, everything was replaced. He handed Elise the new key to replace the old one.

"Is everything secure now?" she asked.

"All clear." He grabbed her in his arms. "Don't worry. We're getting this psycho. I'm not going to let him hurt you."

Chapter Fourteen

Eight Forty-five. Elise jumped into her Pinto. She had to get a move on or she'd be late for her shift at the bookstore. *Fifteen minutes. Not a problem.*

She backed out of the driveway and gave a hesitant wave to Linda who was checking her mailbox. Dang it. They'd probably be back with their invites once they noticed Brad's car in the driveway every night.

That couple was just weird.

Driving up the road, Elise found another reason to groan. There was a scruffy black German Shepherd standing in the middle of the road. He watched her approach and stood his ground as if challenging her.

"Go on, shoo. Shoo, pup." Elise encouraged through the windshield.

The dog didn't move.

That's just great. Where's the owner? She glanced through the windshield for someone. More groaning. There was no one on the sidewalks or in any of the nearby yards that she could see. There's nothing for it. Elise stopped the car and set the emergency flashers.

"All right, buddy. Who do you belong to?" she asked as she got out of the car. Luckily, this street had little traffic so she didn't worry about other cars running her over. But she didn't want this dog to be wandering around, lost. "I haven't seen you before. Are you new?"

"Elise! Oh, Elise, grab her!" A warbling voice called from up the street. Mrs. McGregor, a woman in her eighties, hobbled down the sidewalk as though her legs hurt. Her little feet, shod in white shoes, took tiny, careful steps. "She just ran out the door!" The old woman panted.

Elise walked over to the dog. "Hi sweetheart." Casually, she slipped a finger under the dog's collar, before feeling a jolt of alarm as the dog began to growl.

"Oh, you don't like that." Elise released her. The dog's top lip quivered, giving a white flash of a canine. "Nice puppy." She tried to keep the fear out of her voice as she took a small step back. *This dog is going to attack me. And who's going to help?*

Finally, the elderly woman reached her side. Mrs. McGregor's hands seemed especially fragile as she patted Elsie's arm in gratefulness. "Thank you, dear!"

"Of course." Elise smiled. She wondered how the elderly woman would ever be able to return the big dog to her house. The dog looked like it outweighed the poor woman by twenty pounds.

"Did you get a new dog, Mrs. McGregor?"

"Oh, no. It's my grandson's dog. He just got home from…" the older woman's eyes puddled up, "from a treatment facility. But, he's doing so good now."

"Oh, I'm glad! That's lovely to hear!"

"He's been staying with us recently." She was pink and still out of breath from her trek down the sidewalk. She shook an arthritic finger at the dog. "Oh, Dinah. Naughty girl. How could you?"

The dog tipped her head at her name and gave a doggy smile.

"You need help getting her back to the house?" Elise asked. Mrs. McGregor lived on the corner about five houses down.

"No, dear. I brought her leash." Mrs. McGregor snapped it on and tried to lead her to the sidewalk. Dinah sat as though an immovable statue.

"Oh, poo. Come on!" Mrs. McGregor coaxed.

Elise didn't know how to help, seeing how the animal reacted when she touched her.

"Dinah! Come!" Finally, the muscular dog stood and followed the old woman.

"Thank you again, Elise!" Mrs. McGregor waggled her fingers in goodbye.

"You're welcome. Have a great rest of your morning," Elise called back.

Well, one good deed done for the day. Let's hope the rest of this day will reap the reward.

***

Elise ended up being a few minutes late after all when she arrived at Capture the Magic. Dave waved from the back of the store and started pouring her a mug of coffee as she walked through the store.

"Sorry, I'm late. I was rescuing a dog." She chucked her purse under the counter.

"No worries. It's not like we're on a major timetable here." Dave slid the mug over. "I heard about the surveillance video from Thomas. How're you doing?"

"I'm good." Elise picked up the mug and held it under her nose. Amazing.

"That's pretty creepy that there was someone else here that day. You didn't see anything? You still feel safe here?"

To answer the first question, she shook her head, and then nodded at the second, laughing a bit at how that must look. She took a sip from the mug and grimaced.

Dave laughed at her expression. "What's the matter?"

"Just needs a little bit of sugar." She reached for a sugar packet. "Maybe two."

"Aww, I'd think you were sweet enough as is."

"Very funny. Seriously, this is good coffee. I can't get enough of this freshly ground stuff."

"Stuff?" Dave snorted. "I'll have you know I roast it myself."

"You do not!" Elise was shocked.

"Yeah, I do. I'm a man of many talents." His eyebrows flickered and she laughed. "Speaking of which," he continued, "I'm doing a reading at the library tonight."

"A reading? What of?" She ripped open a sugar packet and dumped it in, then searched for a stirrer.

He shrugged his large shoulders and stroked his beard, looking slightly bashful. "It's two chapters of the book I'm writing now, *In the Stillness*."

"Oh, my gosh! You're reading your horror book!" Elise's voice went up with excitement. "That's amazing!"

"I'd, uh." He cleared his throat. "I'd love it if you could come."

Elise felt the air drain out of the room. *Is he asking as a friend? More? Don't hurt him.* "I think I might have plans with my boyfriend tonight, but maybe we could both stop by if you want. I'd love to hear it."

His face remained impassive except for a tightening around his eyes. "Cool. It'll be at seven." He sighed. "So, you have a boyfriend, huh?"

117

She looked down at the coffee. They so rarely worked together that it hadn't come up yet. "Yeah. We've been together for a while."

"A while...but no ring?"

Elise glanced down at her ring finger and laughed. "No. No ring. Not for a long time."

"He's not the right one, huh?"

Elise raised her eyebrows, slightly taken aback. "I mean, I'm in no rush."

"Can't believe a gal like you hasn't already been taken off the market."

"Well, I was off the market at one point. Marriage didn't work out too well for me." She tried to change the subject. "How about you?"

He tipped the stool back. It squeaked under him as he rested against the wall. Then he came forward with a thump. "I'm looking for a special type. Someone who loves books. *Alice in Wonderland*." He chuckled, then seemed to get serious. "Hey, if it doesn't work out with the boyfriend, let me know."

"Oh, I'm pretty high maintenance. I like long walks, long talks. And lots of good food and wine."

He smiled, laugh wrinkles crinkling around his dark eyes. "Sounds like my kind of woman."

"Except for the boyfriend part." She raised her eyebrows to remind him.

"I've always been a day late and a dollar short," he sighed.

❊ ❊ ❊

Dave made his exit a few minutes after the conversation ended, still insisting he'd like her to stop by at the library. She considered it for a moment—it might be fun to forget everything that was going on and just have a normal date with Brad—until she remembered Brad was working the swing shift. But she wasn't going to let Dave know that, not wanting to be roped into coming alone.

Elise drew a feather duster over the last shelf of books in the Thriller row. Although Dave had never asked her to do it, or even seemed to notice the dust, she'd been diligently working through each of the shelves all week. This place was special and needed a little more upkeep then the bachelor seemed to notice.

She dragged the duster along the cornice of the shelf before backing up, accidentally bumping into the empty stand behind her. A flush of guilt filled her as she looked at it. She'd forgotten to ask Dave how he was doing, or if there were any more leads to the missing book.

The glass had been taken into evidence, leaving just the pillow to sit there on the wood looking empty and forlorn.

Something caught her eye. She leaned in for a closer look. Reflecting the overhead light, an object was stabbed into the wood next to the pillow.

It hadn't been there the day before, of that she was sure. It looked like an especially long, evil pin. She almost pried it out for a closer inspection when that voice inside her curbed her action. *Don't do it. Fingerprints!*

What the heck was it? She walked around the pedestal trying to get a better angle. Maybe it was something found by Dave when he was cleaning. He might have stumbled across it on the floor and stabbed it in here for safe-keeping.

Elise thought about the bearded man. Him? Clean? She shook her head. Doubtful.

Still, she needed to ask.

She walked back to the counter to get her phone from her purse and quickly dialed her bosses number.

He answered on the first ring. "Elise! You calling to take me up on my offer after all?"

"I still have to get back to you on that, but I did want to ask you something."

"I figured since you called." He laughed at his joke.

Elise bit back a groan and forged ahead. "I was just dusting and saw something weird on the book pedestal."

The mood on his end instantly grew somber as he let out a heavy sad sigh.

"We'll get the book back. I'm sure of it," Elise hurried to comfort. "But, in the meantime, there's a giant pin stuck in the wood. Did you do that?"

"What? No, not me."

Elise straightened, a bit surprised at having what she thought was true be confirmed. "Oh, okay. You think it was a customer? Maybe they found it on the floor?"

"A big pin? Like what do you mean?"

Elise walked back over to the display. Her footsteps echoed loudly, underscoring how alone she was.

She started to describe it. "It's got a silver head that looks like it's a filigree ball, and it's about seven inches long."

There was a pause on the other end of the phone.

"Hello? Dave?"

"I'm thinking. It sounds like a hat pin. A very old one by the way you're describing it."

"Okay, a hat pin. That's weird. Why do you think it's old?"

"The length. There was actually a law passed in 1908 over that. People used to be afraid they'd be used as weapons by women suffragettes."

"Seriously?" Elise studied the pin. It really was a beautiful thing. She sucked in her breath. Scratched lightly into the wood next to the pin was a little heart. The initials EP were in the heart. There was an arrow that went right through the initials.

Her initials.

"Uh," her mouth felt dry as she continued. "This just got a little weirder. Um. My initials are carved next to the pin."

"Whoa!" Dave's yell nearly broke her eardrum. "Don't touch anything. I'm coming right back."

"Should I call the police?" she asked. No answer. He'd hung up and was probably already screeching in a U-turn before she destroyed any evidence.

She sighed and texted Brad. **Hey, sweetie. I think I found a clue. Good news- I haven't touched it. Dave is on his way down to examine it.**

He texted back immediately. **Take pictures of it.**

I'm already on it. She scrolled for the camera and snapped a picture. Thoughtfully, she studied the heart again. Who had done this? Were they watching her now?

She shivered and ran back to the front of the store.

❊ ❊ ❊

Five minutes, Dave arrived. He gave her a wave as he strode to the display case. "Wow, that's crazy," he said, examining it. He stroked his beard and shook his head. "Well, there go my plans to read tonight."

"What?" Elise said, startled.

"Detective Sloan just called and wants me to stay until he takes this into evidence."

"I'm sure he'll be here soon," Elise suggested hopefully. "You have all day."

"I'm the kind of person that when I'm told something will be delivered between eight am and six pm, it won't come until nine pm."

"Maybe it won't happen this time."

"What did I tell you earlier about my luck?" He repeated the words as she said them. "A day late and a dollar short."

Chapter Fifteen

Dave knew how nervous Elise was around Detective Sloan and had given her the rest of the day off. "No use in both of us waiting around here." He smiled at her. "Unless you want to stay with me."

Elise had laughed at the joke—at least she hoped it was a joke—and spent the day trying to regroup at her beloved Angel Lake. She'd walked the trails all afternoon, and made plans with Lavina for later. And, as a bonus, Brad would be able to meet for dinner during his swing shift.

She loved the lake. It was her favorite place as a child —a faithful friend whose fragrant breezes swept away her fears, grassy hillside providing a place to study the clouds, as the splash of waves on the beach soothed her thoughts. She always left feeling grounded again.

The lake didn't fail her today, and there was more than a tinge of reluctance when she finally had to leave to get cleaned up.

Back to real life.

An hour later, Elise met Brad at their favorite steak house. "Did the glass pipe ever end up being a clue?" Elise asked Brad over a salad. Her heart warmed as she watched him. Lucy was spending the night with a friend from school. It'd been so long since they'd been alone.

Even him doing something as ordinary as cutting steak and having a regular conversation made her feel all sappy. *What a good guy he is. He's never even complained about having to suddenly share me with a young teenager.*

"What?" he asked, his hazel eyes lit up when he caught her stare.

"I just love you."

He reached over and grabbed her hand and brought it over for a kiss. His thumb rubbed the back of her hand. "Me too, baby. It's nice to have this time together."

"I know. And I just ruined it by asking about the pipe."

Brad chuckled, "No. It's kind of important. Hopefully, the pipe's not one of the boys'. They might be in some trouble."

"What do you mean?"

"Forensics tested it for residue. That wasn't an ordinary pipe."

"Crack?"

"Look's like." He wiped his mouth and proceeded to fork another bite in.

"Oh, man. I hope it doesn't belong to Thomas or Jake."

"Maybe it was one of the bankers'."

"Hey! That might have contributed to Steve's death."
Another hopeful thing! She just needed to keep lining up
the evidence until she was in the clear.

"Could be. It definitely stirs the pot of Detective
Sloan's theories."

"You know I'm a pot stirrer." Elise mimed a swirling
spoon.

"When it comes to collecting evidence you sure are.
Let's see what you've collected so far." He lifted a finger.
"One — an antique pin." He arched an eyebrow. "With a
heart around your initials."

Elise shook her head. "Creepy."

"Proof that everyone who meets you loves you. Two
—" he continued, his second finger up. "Your secret-
admirer's letter." He took a sip of his soda. "And I have
news about that, by the way."

"What?" Elise asked.

"The handwriting expert says the note was written by
the same person who left the note on your car with the
picture."

"How could she tell?"

"He has a 'tell.' His P's have a slight tail at the bottom.
And I noticed it in the picture of the heart you snapped."

"Brad. I don't know how you stick with me. A suspect
for a murder with a crazy stalker involved somehow.

New kid in tow." She wrinkled her nose. "And there's one more thing."

"There's more?" His voice held a note of incredulousness.

She nodded. "Our neighbors—the crazy new ones?—want to have a barbecue or play games or something with us. In fact, they're practically insisting."

"That makes them crazy?" He smiled. "I used to think it meant I was popular when people wanted me to come over."

"No. They're crazy because something is going on with them. I swear he was flirting with me the other day. And I think she might be having an affair."

"Ahh," Brad nodded with a sage look. "They're swingers. Sounds interesting."

"Oh, my gosh!" Elise threw her napkin at him.

"Children!" Lavina breezed up to the table, followed by a dark-haired woman. "Can't take you two anywhere."

"Hey! How are you?" Brad said. He glanced at his watch and stood up. "So, now that your company is here I'm going to head back to work."

"Are we running you out?" Lavina asked Brad as he wiped his mouth and pushed in his chair.

"Nope. I was on my way out. You girls have fun." He leaned down to kiss Elise. Then, with a nod to the other women, he headed out.

"Well, darlin', it does seem that we've interrupted a date," Lavina toned as she settled into a chair. She arranged her purse and jacket next to her. "Elise, this is my friend, Maisie."

The dark-haired woman sat across from them with a smile directed at Elise. She looked extremely elegant and well-dressed in a pearl-colored suit. "Hi, there." She offered her hand over Brad's discarded plate.

At the sight of the new patrons, the waitress hurried over to clean away the dishes. "Can I get you two anything?" she asked Lavina.

"I'd like a pot of hot tea," Lavina glanced at Maisie.

"I'd like a cherry coke."

"I'll be right back with those and bring some menus." The waitress scooted away.

"Well, darlin', tell me all your good gossip." Lavina turned to Elise and waited expectantly.

"Ugh. It seems I have a stalker now."

"You *are* joking." She stared at Elise for a moment, her thickly mascaraed eyes wide with shock. Finding that Elise was not joking, she brought a manicured hand to her forehead as though trying to prevent a headache.

"My, my. You certainly do like to keep things interesting. What am I ever going to do with you?"

The waitress was back and Lavina accepted her tea. The two women ordered salads and then returned to the conversation.

"A stalker!" Maisie said. She shook her head, her dark hair pulled sleekly back into a chignon.

"You can start wearing stilettos," Lavina suggested.

Elise arched an eyebrow. "And why is that?"

"Well, then you always have a weapon on you! Right at your feet."

"I'm more likely to kill myself wearing them." Elise rolled her eyes and looked at Maisie. "Sorry to hog the spotlight. I'd love to hear more about you."

"Well, my story is not as exciting as yours, but I seem to have picked up a stalker myself on Facebook," Maisie said before taking a sip of her soda. "Though I'm not sure he even earns that title. More like a wannabe."

"Really? Who is he? Anyone I know?" Lavina asked.

"Someone from college. He used to live here years ago, but I'm not sure you'd remember him." Maisie pulled out a rhinestone-phone and logged in. "Oh my. He's just liked every picture of mine in…" she scrolled, "the last three months." She showed the two other woman the row of red notifications.

A line formed between Lavina's eyebrows as her mouth opened in astonishment. "I'm thinking he might have been promoted from wannabe to at least faux-stalker."

Maisie studied the phone. "Maybe. Although, he never did have high aspirations. I should have known better than to accept his friend request. And the personal messages he sends! He thinks I'm the best thing since Swiss cheese."

"Promontory or Manchego might be better cheese descriptions," Lavina advised with a wise look.

Maisie smiled. "Oh, sorry dear. I should have known better to watch my words with a Deli connoisseur in our company. Well, anyway. Back when he lived here, he once left me fifty messages on my answering machine. I warned him then that I was going to choke him until he got that peaceful look on his face. At that point, he did back off." She wrinkled her nose at she glanced back at her phone. "I guess it's time for another talk."

Lavina raised a perfect eyebrow. "Darlin', you should never warn them. Then they have time to come up with a back-up plan."

Elise poured a glass of tea. "Honey?"

Both the other women shook their heads.

"So, how do you two know each other?" Elise asked.

"Well..." Maisie glanced at Lavina.

"Through Mr. G, darlin'.'"

"Oh…" Elise looked at Maisie with new respect and more than a little curiosity.

"Look over there," Lavina nudged Maisie's elbow. "Is that Marty Featherbalm?"

Maisie turned to look. "My goodness, it surely is! And can you believe who she's with."

The three women regarded a couple seated at a circular table near the window. The woman appeared to be in her late forties. She'd squeezed herself into a tight dress that had her ample cleavage front and center. Her hair was frosted and teased until it nearly screamed, "The higher the hair, the closer to God." She tipped her head and laugh heartily at something her male companion had said.

"Just look at her laugh. Bless her heart." Lavina gazed under lowered lashes.

"I believe she thinks it sounds like she's playing a violin with her throat," Maisie chimed in. She took another sip from her Cherry Coke.

"Isn't that Ben McArthur she's with?"

Elise felt out of the loop. She leaned over to whisper to Lavina, "Who are these people?"

"They're part of the benefit circuit." Lavina smiled. "Doesn't he have a significant other?" Juicy gossip was her forte.

"Marty used to date Ben years ago, and I think she still sees him as her territory and her toy and doesn't want to give him up!" Maisie nodded.

"She probably wants to keep this all very hush-hush," Lavina added. She began to rifle through her purse for her compact.

"Please. She's the village foghorn. She knows everyone's secrets before they even know them themselves."

"Ya'll are so mean," Elise laughed.

"Mean. This is not mean. Mean is her walking up to Ben's fiancé at the last gala and saying that she must have a lovely dermatologist because no one could tell she was inching toward sixty," Lavina retorted.

Elise gasped. "She didn't!"

Lavina nodded. "She certainly did. All the while giving her black widow smile and staring daggers." She touched up her lipstick. "But forget about her. Tomorrow is your birthday. How are we going to celebrate?"

Elise groaned. "Get me out of being a murder suspect?"

"Well, darlin'," Lavina's hand paused before pouring the tea from the very decadent china teapot. "First it was me, and now you. We truly are two peas in a pod."

Chapter Sixteen

Elise was the first one in the bookstore the next morning. It was odd to open the door and not smell the coffee already brewing. As she walked toward the back, Dave came running in.

"Hey, Dave," she said, peeling off her sweater and hanging it from the hook on the office door. As soon as she took it off, she second-guessed it, rubbing her hands together. The store was chilly.

"Hi, Elise. Thanks for covering for me."

"Of course!"

"I still feel terrible asking you at the last minute to come in early. But I didn't realize my appointment was for this morning. I had tomorrow on my brain, for some reason."

She laughed and tried to reassure him. "Dude, I work for you. This is my job to cover when you need me. Besides, the earlier shift works out better for me, anyway. It's my birthday and I made some plans for later."

"Your birthday! Great. Now I feel worse. I'd give you the whole day off except for that darn appointment. Just don't work too hard. Keep the cleaning to a minimum. Let's not find any more hat pins."

Elise snorted. "My only goal is to make sure everything goes like it's supposed to," she said, more confident than she felt. So far, nearly every day she'd worked something unexpected had happened.

She was beginning to worry if she wasn't the jinx.

Dave wandered into his office and returned with a folder in his hands. He said as he walked out, "Keep things mellow, okay? I used to joke to my employees about not burning the place down. But for you, it's not a joke. And, Happy Birthday."

She laughed and promised everything would be fine. Because what else could she do?

It was only nine, and the morning sun slanted through the windows and illuminated decades-old dust. She sighed. *I may be losing the battle to clean this place.* Footsteps pounded overhead. She was surprised the Escape room had visitors so early.

Elise opened the dishwasher and began to unload the mugs and coffee parts, setting the espresso machine pieces to one side. That chore done, she refilled the bean hopper from a brown bag that Dave had brought—the roast he was so proud of—and then set to work putting the espresso machine in order.

It's my birthday! She laughed to herself at the giddy bubble of excitement stirring inside. *You'd think I was in junior high.* But she couldn't wait to go horseback riding.

Her quiet thoughts were disturbed by impatient tapping on the counter.

Elise whirled around. Jake stood there, staring at her.

"Hi," she said breathlessly, and straightened up, trying to appear like she hadn't been scared. She hadn't heard him come down the stairs.

He didn't answer her. Instead, he continued to drum his fingers on the counter.

"Is there something you need? Want a coffee?" She set the coffee filter down.

"Advice. I might need advice." On his head sat a top hat, askew.

Odd. First things first. Get rid of the hat.

"Okay." Elise leaned against the counter. "What kind of advice you need? School? Girl?" She smiled at the last word.

The young man didn't smile back. "You think I'm a lot younger than I really am."

Elise straightened. Something about the man's tone didn't sit right with her. She studied him carefully. His pupils were huge and he seemed to be sweating. "You feeling okay? What's with the hat?"

"Yeah. Fine." Jake picked up a cellophane-wrapped cookie. He twirled it in his hand and chuckled. "Just need a cookie I guess." He reached into his pocket and forked over a ragged five dollar bill. It had a weird odor to it and she immediately wrinkled her nose. "And as for the hat, I do run the Escape the Rabbit Hole room. Ever heard of the Mad Hatter?" He opened the cookie and took a bite, bringing attention to the sweat gathering on his upper lip.

The bell above the front door rang, and a police officer walked in. Jake glanced at him, then sharply turned away. His hand scratched at his face. "Keep the change," he muttered then walked towards the door.

Just before he passed the officer, he looked up the stairs. Turning his head slowly, he studied the ceiling until he gave a satisfied grin. Elise followed his gaze — the camera that Dave had replaced. He tipped his hat straighter. Then, lowering his head, he passed the officer. Almost angrily, he slammed the front door.

Elise raised her eyebrows. *Weird.* She picked up the bill and examined it carefully before raising it to her nose. It smelled terrible, like turpentine. She put it in the cash register and counted out the change. After slipping the bills into her pocket, she wiped her hands on her pants. Really, the whole thing made her feel gross for some reason. Crushing really. The pipe *had* to be his.

The officer walked up the counter. He removed his hat, revealing a gray crew-cut. "Elise Pepper?"

She took a deep breath and nodded. *What fresh new disaster is this?*

"I'm Detective Steele. I'd like to ask you a few questions."

"Okay," she grabbed a towel and almost defensively began wiping the counter. "How can I help you?"

"I've been talking with Officer Carter."

Elise nodded. She'd heard of Detective Steele, one of Brad's old partners before he got transferred. So it made sense this was who Brad had been talking with.

"And," he continued. "I need to know if there's anything you haven't mentioned, anything you can think of at all that might help us find the person who's stalking you."

"I've been trying. Trust me, I want to know who it is more than anyone."

"We examined the listening devices. They're pretty elementary, something that could be easily picked up online." He rubbed his ham-sized hand over the top of his bristly head and then stared at her. "You see, we're at a crossroads here, wondering who's doing this."

Elise used Brad's tactic and waited silently, hoping it would lure the Detective into saying more.

"You see, no one knows your house better than you. And it's odd that all these things have been found specifically by you." His eyes narrowed into two dark slits as he considered her.

He's not saying what I think he's saying, is he? And this is Brad's friend? Her heart pounded in her chest. *Don't even blink, Elise.* She crossed her arms in front of her.

"Well, I just wanted to check in and see if you had any news." He replaced his hat. "I guess I'll be seeing you around." He glanced around the bookstore and then back at her. "Don't you worry. We always get our guy."

As soon as he was out of the store, Elise was on the phone with Brad. "Don't worry, baby," he tried to console her. "This is just what they do. I should have warned you."

"Why are you even bringing the evidence to them if they're just going to use it against me?"

"I'll talk to him. He's just covering his bases. I promise, they have nothing on you."

"I can't do this anymore Brad. I'm over it." Elise's eyes stung with threatened tears. Suddenly, she felt so tired.

"Look, I'm coming down to the store and I'll hang out until you're off. And then we'll go celebrate your birthday, okay? We're going to have fun if it's the last thing we do."

She wiped her eyes and nodded before realizing he couldn't see her. "Maybe don't word it that way. And, your right. I just couldn't believe he'd come in here and practically threaten me like he thought I was a liar."

"I know. I'm sorry. This is all going to blow over. Just hang tough." His voice warmed, "I have a surprise for you."

A surprise. Well then. "You know how I like prizes."

His laugh seemed to wrap her in love. "Yeah, you do. And, I've got a good one."

Chapter Seventeen

Later that afternoon, Dave returned to the bookstore. He held his jaw as though it hurt and grimaced as he settled down on the coffee bar stool.

"Oh, no!" Elise exclaimed. "Are you all right? You didn't say your appointment was at the dentist's."

He laughed and moved his hand. "Sorry, I had to tease you. No, it was with my lawyer. We filed an insurance claim on the book." He glanced over at the empty pedestal. "I'm going to miss it, but I guess I'll be getting quite a bit for it."

"Really?" Brad looked impressed. He'd been following Elise around the store all morning as she cleaned, and now relaxed on one of the couches.

"Uh, yeah." Dave appeared startled to see Brad there. He cleared his throat and then continued. "I'm going to get full value and then some for what it would have eventually appreciated for."

"Oh, that's great." Elise inwardly rolled her eyes. *Did you just tell him it was great his book got stolen?* "I mean, I'm sorry you lost such a precious family heirloom, but I'm glad you will have some compensation for it."

"I knew what you meant." He walked to the counter. "And to celebrate, both my news and your birthday, I got you this."

He placed a bag—the kind from a nice clothing store — on the counter and smiled expectantly.

"Oh, my goodness. You totally shouldn't have." Elise reached for the twine handles, feeling slightly awkward.

Dave cut a gaze to Brad, who watched with a relaxed expression, and then back to Elise. "When I saw this in the window, I knew it would be perfect for you. Check it out."

She reached into the bag and withdrew a hat. Bright red and felted, the hat had a small heart edged in jewels on the band.

"Oh, my goodness," she said, hardly knowing how to react. She glanced at his face. He was dead serious. "It's beautiful, Dave."

"The Queen of Hearts," he murmured.

"What was that?" Brad asked.

"The Queen of Hearts. You know, from *Alice in Wonderland*. I wanted to give you a good memory of the story after what happened. I couldn't leave it like it was."

"Aw. Thank you. That was so thoughtful!" She placed the hat on her head and turned to Brad. "Well, this does fit for our date."

"Yeah? Where are we going?"

"Riding horses!"

Brad's dark eyebrows rose quickly. He didn't say anything, but his expression said it all.

She batted her eyes. "Come on. It will be fun. It's for my birthday...."

"Horseback riding? And how is the poor hat involved? That ain't a cowgirl hat."

She reached up to see if it was centered on her head. "You know, fancy hats..."

"That's the Kentucky Derby," Brad said dryly.

Dave laughed.

"All right, close enough." Elise shrugged before carefully placing the hat back in the bag. "Thanks again, Boss."

"You bet. No problem. Now, you two kids go have fun," Dave said, waving them away.

Out in Brad's car, Elise reached for his hand. "Does it sound like fun? Or does the idea of it just totally freak you out?"

Brad's nose flared as he exhaled slowly. He stroked his jaw as if deliberating.

"I mean, we can plan something different if it really bothers you." Elise conceded.

He smiled and shook his head. "Nah. You usually let me pick the movie. I guess I can go do this with you." He raised an eyebrow. "Just this once, though. Okay?"

"Unless you love it. We're going to be riding on a trail by the lake."

Brad didn't seem impressed at this news. "Mph." He already looked like he regretted his decision. "I'll probably get the horse named Diablo."

Elise laughed. "They won't have a horse named that."

"You watch and see," he muttered. "It'll probably try to bite me."

Thirty minutes later, they arrived. The entrance was covered with an arching sign that read, "Grant's Horse Ranch." Brad's fingers nervously drummed against the steering wheel as he pulled down the driveway.

"I guess this is it." He didn't look happy as he parked.

"You sure about this? I don't want to do it unless you feel ready." She hesitated before unbuckling her seatbelt.

"Baby, I was born ready." He raised an eyebrow at her. His mouth turned in that roguish smile she loved. She reached for his neck to pull him in for a kiss, which he gave readily.

"Come on, cowboy. Let's see what you got."

Slowly, they walked up the driveway. Two horses — one black and one brown — were already saddled and waiting outside the stable. Elise noticed a lot of noise over at the main house where the porch lay in shambles. A pair of saw horses had been set up near the house, along with scattered electrical equipment as a construction crew rebuilt the porch.

"Watch out. I'm telling you, that the black one's name is Diablo," Brad whispered while squeezing her hand. Elise smirked.

The black one did appear big and bad enough to be called Diablo, but it was actually the chestnut one that seemed more skittish. Hooves clattered over the gravel-strewn driveway as the horse refused to stand still. The stable hand was stroking its nose and murmuring to calm it down.

"Hi, there," A woman dressed in saddle pants and plaid shirt strode forward, hand outstretched, to greet them. Two helmets hung from their straps in her other hand. "I'm Emily, and that there is Cecil. He'll be the one accompanying you on your ride, today. Here are your helmets, if you could put them on." She handed the over.

"And what's this horse's name?" Brad pointed to the black one. He fastened the helmet in place.

"That one there's name is Festus, and the other is a sweet girl named Lucky."

At her name, the chestnut danced some more.

"What's going on with her, Cecil?" Emily asked the other worker.

"Aw, she's fine. Normally, she's our beginner rider." The young man addressed Elise, as if wanting to reassure her. "They both are. I think she's just anxious to get out on the trail."

Lucky did seem to calm down as Cecil continued to stroke her nose. The stable hand positioned the horse and then beckoned for Elise to climb on. "She doesn't take kindly to men, though, so this will be your ride."

Elise buckled on her helmet and tried to tamp down her growing feeling of apprehension. She patted the horse's neck and felt a jolt of apprehension as the hide of the horse shivered under her touch. "Are you sure she's okay?"

"She's fine. Aren't you, darlin'?" Cecil rubbed noses with the horse. "She's a sweetie pie."

Elise stuck her foot into the stirrup and grabbed the saddle horn. With a decidedly unladylike grunt, she pulled herself up. The horse stirred under her for a moment and then settled back down. But Elise could feel the horse's tension like a live wire.

She stroked Lucky's neck again. "Good girl. You're a good girl, aren't you?" Elise looked up to see Emily had talked Brad up on his horse and Cecil had mounted a pinto.

"Keep the reins nice and loose." Cecil rode over to Brad's side and loosened the reins. "That's right. Just a light touch is all that's needed. Now, both of you go ahead and use your heels a bit to get the horses moving."

Elise gently bumped the horse's belly with her heels. That's when the world spun upside down.

Chapter Eighteen

"Whoa! Whoa!" Elise screamed. The horse bucked and twisted. Brad leaped off his horse and reached for hers. Lucky danced away from his outstretched hands. Cecil rode over to corral her, but Lucky bucked away.

The next thing Elise knew, the horse was running. Ears back, neck outstretched, Lucky's hooves ate up the trail and sent the gravel flying. Elise hunkered over the horse's neck and hung on for dear life.

Surprisingly, the horse's gait was smooth. That wasn't the problem. The problem was the horse wasn't responding to the reins or showing any intention of slowing down.

Elise craned her neck to look ahead, squinting as the wind made her eyes tear. Her hand gripped the saddle horn tighter as she saw the path veered around a large oak. The horse seemed to be aiming straight for the tree.

In a flash, Elise realized exactly what was about to happen. The horse was going to scrape her off on the oak like she was a tick.

Elise grabbed the horse by the mane. "Whoa, Lucky! Whoa!"

All she could see was the whites of the horse's eyes. Wild eyes. Scared eyes.

The horse jumped over a log. Elise's teeth clattered together, nearly causing her to bite her tongue in half. She gritted her jaw and yanked harder on the reins.

One sharp limb from the tree pointed in her direction, ready to spear her if she couldn't get the horse to stop.

A brown and white blur appeared by her side. Cecil. His horse was neck and neck with her own. The stablehand didn't bother with the reins, but instead reached across and looped his arm around her waist. With a swift yank, he pulled her free from the saddle. She swung her leg over his horse and grabbed tightly around him. Tears of relief burned her eyes.

Cecil slowed his pinto as the two of them watched Lucky continue to race away. More hoof noises sounded behind them. Whipping past, Emily flew by on her roan after the run-away horse. The two horses disappeared around the corner.

"You okay?" Cecil's voice was shaky. He turned to look at her, his eyes wide with panic.

"Just let me down. I need to get down now." Shaking, Elise started to swing her leg around. Cecil held out his arm to brace her. Her legs nearly collapsed as her feet touched the ground.

The horse took a few steps as Cecil turned the pinto around. "I have no idea what just happened. She's never acted that way before."

Elise rubbed her face and breathed deeply. *You're okay. No need to cry now.* "Well, just my luck," she said. Clouds of dust hung in the air from the mad-dash she'd just been on.

She began to walk back to the stable.

Cecil rode next to her. "You want up again?"

"Not really." *Like never again. Romanticizing horse riding officially cured.*

"I know that had to scare you, but I'd sure like to see you get back on the horse again. I'll even lead. This one won't run. I promise."

"Since I have no idea what I did to make the other horse so crazy, I think I'll pass," Elise said, matter-of-factly. She unbuckled her helmet. The wind picked up and blew her hair across her face. She shivered and crossed her arms as it cooled her perspiring skin.

Half-way down the path she met Brad. His face was grim, his lips set in two determined lines. When she saw him, the teary-feeling bubbled up again and she ran to his arms.

He grabbed her, whispering words she couldn't really hear. She snuggled into his strength, never wanting him to let go.

Finally, he pushed her away and took a hard look at her. He brushed the hair from her face and a half-smile crooked his mouth. "You never did like to do anything half-way. Always having to blow the expectations away."

"I'm never getting on a horse again," she declared adamantly.

"Sure you are. Just not today. I don't think I could take it if you raced away from me again." He held his hand over his heart dramatically. "I think that cut like ten years off of my life. I'm officially traumatized and Diablo didn't even do it. My girlfriend did." He wrapped his arm around her waist as they continued back to the stable.

The clips of hooves made them glance back. Emily was leading Lucky. The chestnut still looked a little skittish but the stable hand had a firm grip on the reins. She led the horse passed them. "Come on, Cecil. Let's get our girl in her stall. I'll meet you two there," she threw over her shoulder at Brad and Elise.

Ten minutes later, Brad and Elise made it back to the stable. Not seeing anyone but the construction workers, they peeked into the barn.

The fresh smell of hay and animals greeted them. Lucky was in her stall appearing considerably calmer. Another stable hand was filling her water bucket while Cecil and Emily stood together looking at something in the square of sunlight that spilled through the door.

"Hi, guys," Brad said as they walked over.

Emily held something in her fingers as Cecil flashed a guilty look.

Brad picked up on it immediately. "What's going on? What'd you find?"

Emily glanced at Cecil before answering. "We took off Lucky's gear and found this woven in one of the stirrups." The stablehand held it out—something thin and shiny.

Elise covered her mouth as she realized what it was.

A hat pin.

"Honest, we have no idea how that got in there," Cecil blathered quickly. "I've never seen anything like it."

"Let me see it." Brad held out his hand. Emily deposited the pin.

It was nearly identical to the last one in length, but the head on this one was a pearl.

Brad turned it over. "Did you see anything else on the saddle? Any words scratched in the leather?"

The two stablehands shook their heads as Brad reached for his phone. His hazel eyes swept over Elise sympathetically. "I have to call this in."

Elise nodded.

"Sorry about your birthday." He kissed her. "We'll make up for it tomorrow."

"If this is how my birthday started, I'm a little worried about the rest of the year."

He smiled. "I still have my gift to give you." The smile dropped off as the person on the other line answered. "Hello? Detective Steele? There's been an attempt on Elise's life."

Chapter Nineteen

"An attempt on my life?" Elise sat in her window seat with her head against the window sill. "I can't even believe it." Her eyes were closed as she listened to Adele blaring through the stereo. A thump on the cushion made her open them again as Max butted her leg. "You like this song, buddy? This is my jam."

The orange cat closed his eyes and swished his tail hard.

"Oh, a snobby one, eh? Don't judge me." She scratched his head.

A flutter outside the glass caught her eye. A bird was building its nest in the cherry tree just outside her window. It landed on a twig and turned its head toward her, one dark eye sparkling. A bit of grass dangled from its beak. It tucked the grass into its nest then, like a flash, it was off.

She looked over at the neighbors', and couldn't help the way her mouth twisted to the side in distaste. *Oh crap. There he is by his car.* Just then, Seth noticed her and waved. As if to emphasize he saw her, he winked and made a shooting motion with his index finger pointed in her direction.

What the heck does that mean?

She scooted from the window and turned down the stereo. So far, she'd been able to wiggle her way out of their invitations for a game night. But how much longer? It seemed like they constantly watched for an opportunity to corner her. Yesterday, Seth had trapped her at the mailbox. Luckily, she'd been able to use her birthday as an excuse out of a long conversation.

Just what she needed right now, weird, possibly psycho neighbors watching her every move. *They weren't really psycho, were they? Why do I keep attracting these types of people?*

At least Lucy was doing well at school. Her mom was still in rehab and seemed to be really fighting for recovery for the first time. Lucy had been through it before and still hung on to her skepticism. Elise hoped, for the teen's sake, that the mom would make good on her promises this time. Summer would be here soon, and the state would reassess the foster care situation then.

What would Elise say to Lucy's mom when they finally met? Half of her wanted to punch the woman right in the face for allowing a situation where her boyfriend pawed over her teenage daughter, leaving poor Lucy with the only choice but to run away and try to make it on the streets.

The other half wanted to try and rescue the mom, too.

I'll worry about that later. If I'm not in jail myself. Elise's eyelids fluttered closed. *Dear Lord. I just want a normal life.*

She replayed the race on the horse and the two hat pins. What did the pins mean? What about the note? How did this all correlate with *Alice in Wonderland*?

This is connected. I know it is. Elise reached for her phone and opened the browser. She typed in **Alice in Wonderland**, shivering with anticipation at what would come up.

At the first picture, she covered her mouth. Of course. How could she be so stupid? The cartoon figure leered at her, looking silly and at the same time menacing. As a little girl, she'd laughed at him.

And his silly tea parties.

The Mad Hatter. Now the sight of him sent a chill straight to her bones. The hat pins were a warning more menacing than a cartoon figure could bring. And, the recent murder in the escape room had only emphasized just how mad.

She thought about the poem she'd received, framed by the weird drawing.

Tic-Toc the clock's about to stop.
What if Alice never returned from the rabbit hole?
Would she, could she have married?
The hare may be calling her back.

So, what happens when the Mad Hatter thinks he's in love with someone? What does he do if that person doesn't return his affections?

She clicked on a link titled 'The March Hare' and scrolled through the next pictures. Her eyes widened. There were the same vines that the stalker had drawn on the laughing flowers of her note.

But in this cartoon, the vines had twisted up around Alice until she hung from the air by her neck.

❃ ❃ ❃

"You just searched this up?" Brad asked. He glanced at her, his face creased with concern.

"I did. And there's something more. A few days ago someone wrote in the dust in my car—Elise in Wonderland."

"Why didn't you tell me about this sooner?" His eyes narrowed with frustration. "You can't keep stuff away from me like that."

"Honestly, I completely forgot. So much happened that day, and really every day since. I'm telling you now." She gave him a winning smile.

"I spent all day with you yesterday," he said dryly.

"As if nothing happened to distract me," she said back just as dry. She smiled again. "But I remember today and put it together. So there's that. And I took a picture." She fumbled with her phone to show him.

"This isn't a joke," he said, glancing at it. "You've actually had a threat against your life."

"Well, I don't know about *my* life. I mean, how did the guy know I was going to ride that horse? It could have just as easily been you."

Brad pressed his lips together. "I've already thought about that."

Elise raised her eyebrows. "You have? And what did you come up with?"

"That someone might have been trying to get rid of me to have you all to themselves."

Elise felt sick to her stomach at the thought.

"So do you have any idea at all who could be doing this?" Brad asked.

"I wish you would stop that."

"Stop what?"

"Stop asking me as if I haven't been thinking about it. Don't you realize I've been wracking my brain trying to figure out who it is?"

"Look, it's not your fault this is happening. But sometimes the stalker is someone the person is very familiar with. I'm just trying to get you to look at each relationship and see if you notice any red flags."

"Well," Elise hesitated. "I was thinking it might be the new neighbor."

"Why do you think it's him?"

"Besides the creepy things I've already told you? I just don't trust him. He's always watching me." Elise frowned at the memory of just that morning, her eyes automatically looking out the window. "It's probably silly."

"So what if it's silly?" Brad crossed his arms, the blue flannel shirt creasing at the elbows. "But here's something I know about you, Elise. You have very good instincts. Don't doubt yourself."

Elise tried to put into words what her intuition was telling her. "It's like when I first met them. Seth didn't act like I was a stranger. He looked at me like he knew me from somewhere."

"Knew you enough to write you a letter?" Brad's face was grim. "He's someone who can see you coming and going. And it would have been easy for him to snap a picture or leave a letter in your mailbox."

Elise wrinkled her nose. "Except...."

"Except what?" Brad pressed.

"Lucy had said it was someone in a brown truck that had left the letter. And it doesn't explain the hat pins."

"Not every question is going to be answered when I get that guy." Brad's hands squeezed into fists. "And what if it's Dave, huh? Have you thought about that?"

"Yes." Elise nodded. "But my gut tells me he's a good guy. A little lonely, but sincere."

"Yeah, well, whoever he's is, I'm bringing him down. He's messed with the wrong woman."

Chapter Twenty

Elise awoke from a dream—or was it a nightmare?—where teacups chased one another as sugar cubes were hurled from a giant metal ladle. Her bedroom door creaked—for the second time, Elise realized—and slowly opened. Every muscle in her body tensed to spring into action.

"Elise?" The whispered words were urgent and laced with fear. "Elise are you awake?"

Lucy. Elise fell back in relief. Reaching over, she checked that her golf club was still standing by the side of the bed, her small nod to protecting herself since Brad had to work the midnight shift tonight.

She tried to sit up, but her legs were trapped in twisted blankets. Too late, she realized Max had also been pinning them down. He stared with disdain from the spot where he'd been rudely transferred to at the end of the bed before licking his paw. Then, without a look back, he jumped to the floor and flounced from the room.

The door was a dark crack with the shadowy figure of the teen clinging to the frame.

"Lucy? Come in! Are you okay?"

"N-no," came the wavering reply.

"What's wrong?" When only a sniffle was returned, Elise reached out her arms. "Lucy, come here."

The teen didn't need to be asked again. The pale figure dashed across the room, her bare foot visible for a moment in the rectangle of moonlight on the floor. She jumped on the bed, half landing on Elise, who let out a "Whump!"

Lucy didn't quit wiggling until she'd buried herself under the comforter and curled her cold body against Elise's. As Elise drew her arm around the teen, Lucy pressed her face against her shoulder. Tears dampened Elise's t-shirt as the teen's body shivered. "What's going on, sweetie? Did you have a nightmare?"

Lucy didn't answer, but Elise felt the nod against her neck. She held the girl and waited for her to collect herself enough to speak. Finally, soft, faltering words came out.

"I'm afraid of the neighbor."

"Seth?" Elise felt a wave of anger. *What has he done?* "I'll kill him. What did he do to you?"

"No. Linda." Lucy shivered again. "I've seen her outside my school twice now. And sometimes, she just stands at the end of the driveway and stares."

Elise's mouth dropped open. "What? She does not."

At this, Lucy pushed away. Her hair was sweaty and her eyes swollen. "She does! I swear it!"

"No. No, Lucy. I believe you. I was just expressing shock. What does she do after she stands there?"

"The last time, she took a picture and typed something on her phone and then walked back to her house." Lucy sat up and wiped her shirt sleeve down her cheek. "I don't know what's going on with them but they creep me out." She sniffed hard. "And then there's that white truck. It's always over there."

"What do you mean? You've seen it at their house, again?"

"Yes. Every night, it's parked there while you're making dinner. And it leaves about an hour later."

"Right before Brad gets here." Elise closed her eyes as slow fury began to build inside of her at the thought of Linda. *Harass my girl? Oh, you've had it now.*

"And her husband." Lucy sniffed again.

Elise rolled her eyes. Good grief. Was the whole world going crazy? "Come here," she said to Lucy, scooting the girl closer and hugging her tighter. "I am so sorry. I thought we solved you having to face any weirdness by having you go home with your friend after school. Do you want to come to the bookstore instead?"

"No. I'm okay. I just wanted to let you know. I couldn't quit thinking about it tonight."

"You just need a break. We need to get you out of here. There's way too much going on, with the pictures, letters, and now crazy neighbors. You want to hang out with Lavina? I bet she can make all of this better."

Elise could see Lucy smiled a tiny bit by the moonlight. "Lavina?"

"Yes! She'd love to have you. Oh, my gosh. I'm not sure if she won't give you a makeover or two, but it'll be a good time."

Lucy twisted her hair around her finger as a wistful look came on her face. "A makeover?"

The look gripped Elise's heart. With everything that had been going on, had she neglected Lucy? The poor girl probably needed to do more girl things, things Elise never had been good at. Like walking in high heels, makeup, and knowing what purse went with which outfit. "Yes, a make-over. She's always threatening to do one on me. Maybe she can teach you some stuff and you can help me later. Would you like that?"

Lucy nodded shyly.

"Okay, then. It's settled. I'll call Lavina."

"All right, Elise." Lucy snuggled into her pillow and gave a happy sigh. "This is the best thing ever."

"What's the best thing? A makeover?"

Lucy giggled. "That'll be fun. But, seriously, I can't even tell you. It's the best thing ever to be taken care of. To know I'm safe. I can't even express how awesome that is. It's a first time for me."

Elise swallowed hard at the lump in her throat. Every girl should know what it feels like to feel safe. It should be such a staple that you only notice when it's missing, not when it's given. "Well, good. I'm impressed with how you've always known how to keep yourself safe, and now you know there are others who will stand with you, too. You aren't alone anymore."

A contented little hum came from Lucy who tugged the covers up to her chin. Elise studied her for a moment. *Okay then, I guess she's sleeping here tonight.*

Within moments, heavy, slow breathing indicated Lucy was out. Elise marveled at how quickly the teen fell asleep. Max rejoined them with a leap on the bed. He yawned, his canines glittering in the moonlight, before curling up into an orange ball. His tail covered his nose as he shut his eyes.

Just me awake, I guess. The cheese stands alone. Elise scooted to the edge of the bed and tucked the pillow under her head. It was kind of cramped, with Max weighing down the blankets. She wasn't used to sharing her bed. Still, there was something peaceful about having those two sleep so sweetly that lent itself to peace for her too.

In her old life, a million years ago, she never would have thought that happiness could look like scattered shoes and clothing in place of bubble baths with glasses of wine, homework questions in place of socializing with the other attorney wives, or a cramped double bed filled with content sleepers in place of a king size and 1000 count sheets. *Where I'd always slept alone...*

Home. Family. It definitely wasn't what she'd expected all those years ago, but now she wouldn't trade it for anything. She smiled as she closed her eyes and fell asleep.

Chapter Twenty-One

The next day at work, Elise tried to work out the best way to confront Linda. It was hard to think straight through the fury that kept flaring up. *How dare she. Standing in front of Lucy's school? Taking pictures of her at home? Really? What was she doing there?*

Maybe she suspects her husband is at my house.

But why would Linda care about that when she so obviously had someone at *her* house every day?

"You okay?" Dave asked, after she knocked over a stack of books she'd been unboxing.

"I'm fine." Her words came out more terse than she meant.

"You seem a little distracted. What's going on?" He poured fresh coffee beans into the grinder, filling the store with their oily scent. "Boyfriend?" He looked at her sympathetically, but Elise saw a flicker of hopefulness in his eyes.

"No, Brad and I are fine. It's neighbor problems."

"Ahh. Fighting over property lines? Where to put the fence?"

Elise unpacked a few more books from the box and shook her head.

"Let me guess. Your dog is using their yard when he goes outside."

"Nope. You're horrible at this game. And I don't have a dog."

"Your cat, then."

Elise paused to consider this. Was it possible all this weirdness was over Max digging in their garden? "Maybe...." she conceded. "I need to talk to her."

"Talk to the neighbor—that doesn't sound like it's going to end well. I'm pretty sure I've read at least one murder mystery that started that way." He shook his head. "You know what they say?"

"What?"

"Tall fences make for good neighbors."

Elise laughed. "Well, in this case, she lives across the street, so a fence wouldn't help. And what would you know, anyway? Mr. Town home living?"

"As soon as I pull into my parking spot, I put on a stone-cold face that says I'm a jerk. No one talks to me." He demonstrated an emotionally-devoid face and lowered his eyebrows in a scowl.

"Ah!" Elise said, pretending to shrink back.

"See!" His grin popped back and he replaced the lid on the grinder. "Works every time."

A chime indicated Elise had a text. "Do you mind?" she asked Dave.

"Go for it." He waved his hand. "I've got some writing to do, anyway." He headed into his office.

She pulled her phone from under the counter. It was from Lavina.

Darlin, send that girl right over!

It was an answer to one of Elise's earlier texts about Lucy.

Elise wrote back—**Thanks so much. Life is kind of crazy here**

When is it not?

Elise sent back a frowny face.

Can I take her shopping? —was Lavina's response.

If you want. I'm sure she'll love that.

Can I get her hair done? Lavina, again.

If she'll let you. Elise remembered the wistful look on Lucy's face and thought there's no way she'd turn a trip to the salon down. Poor girl.

Lavina sent back an emoji shower of lipstick, hearts and high heels. Elise grinned as she sent Lucy a text confirming that she needed to go to Lavina's deli after school. Then, she sent one to Brad letting him know that she had something important to talk to him about at dinner.

His response came back right away—**Okay....now I'm worried. And I still have your birthday gift to give you**

Elise couldn't blame him. But maybe he'd have some ideas on how to approach the neighbors. She smiled at the thought of the gift.

"Hey, I almost forgot. This came for you earlier," Dave said, sliding over an envelope on the counter.

The envelope was soft yellow and the size of a birthday card. Elise picked it up and examined the address. Elise Pepper c/o Capture the Magic Bookstore.

The hairs on the back of her neck prickled.

The P's all had decidedly curly tails.

There was a return address in the corner. Charles L. Dodgson, Cheshire, England. The stamp was a postage-paid red-inked seal.

England? What in the world? She slid her finger under the flap and carefully opened it.

Happy Birthday! Were the first words she read. Inside, in scrawling print, it asked, "Did you like your new hat pin? The pearl was inspired by a poem about the Walrus and the Carpenter. I hope you've read it and love it as much as I do."

I'm going to throw up.

"Did you say something?" asked Dave.

Elise grabbed the counter, suddenly feeling dizzy. She hadn't realized she'd said those words out loud. "Dave, I'm sorry. I'm not feeling well."

He came hurrying from his office, his eyebrows raised with concerned. "You okay?"

"Dave, have you ever heard of a poem about a Walrus and a Carpenter?"

"Oh small one, you are speaking of *Alice in Wonderland* lore." He grinned, pleased to share his knowledge. "It's about a walk that a Walrus and a Carpenter took on the beach, along with a bunch of trusting oysters."

"Why were the oysters trusting?" Elise was afraid to hear the answer.

"They thought the Walrus and Carpenter were friends. But instead, the two of them ate the oysters all up."

Bile rose up Elise's throat and she shook her head. "I think I'm going to throw up. I might need to go home."

"Oh, geez. You don't look so hot." He walked over and felt her forehead. "No fever. Are you okay to drive?"

"Yeah. I just—I just need to get home." Elise looked at him desperately. "I'm sorry."

"Of course! No problem. Just call tomorrow and let me know how you're doing."

Elise nodded gratefully and grabbed her purse and the card. "Thank you, Dave. I really appreciate it."

"Sure thing. Go take care of yourself."

Out in the car, Elise tried to call Brad. No answer. She texted him — **Brad, Everything's fine but call me asap.**

She didn't say anymore, needing to talk to him in person. He was working his beat and she'd never forgive herself if something happened to him because he was distracted by her.

Nausea continued to roil in her stomach. Elise swallowed repeatedly. She glanced at the card sitting next to her on the passenger seat. It looked so innocent, the front decorated with a deck of cards and the words, "I'm all in."

How had he found out it was her birthday? Just how close was this guy?

An idea came to her. *I'm so blind. All this time I figured it was a man. But what if... it's a woman?*

Elise drove home, churning that idea over in her head. She'd just about talked herself out of it when she turned down the road to see Linda, the neighbor, standing in the center of her driveway.

Chapter Twenty-Two

Linda stared her down as Elise pulled into the driveway. The young neighbor's hands were on her hips.

"What are you doing here?" Elise demanded as she got out. She slammed the door to emphasize how angry she was.

"I've been needing to talk with you." Linda tipped her chin, appearing as if she was challenging her.

"You're here because you need to talk with me? There's no way you could have known I was coming home. What are you doing?"

"I was going to stick a note on your door." Linda's voice held a defensive tone.

Elise quickly examined the woman's hands. There was no note.

"Just give me a minute of your time. It's important," Linda began again.

"I don't know who you are," Elise said, backing up to the front door. "Or what you and your kooky husband want, but you leave me alone. I'm contacting the police about you harassing my niece."

"She's not your niece." Linda's comment was snide. She smiled, obviously pleased she caught Elise off-guard.

Elise was so shocked she didn't notice the edge of the walkway. Her heel caught in the flower bed and she fell backward.

"Here, let me help you," Linda said. She eased forward.

"No! Get away from me!" Elise jumped up. "You just stay there. I know all about the help you want to give."

"I do want to help you."

"Right. By helping to install more bugs in my house? Maybe send a few more letters and pictures?"

"What do you mean?" Linda edged a little bit closer, cutting between Elise and her car.

"Or maybe you want to stand at the end of my driveway and stare at us some more." Elise held her arms out defensively.

Linda glanced at the house next door. "Can you please just calm down. Let's go inside and talk." She slipped her hand into her pocket. There was something bulky in there and her slim form seemed to grow with the threat.

Dear Lord, she has a gun.

"Stop!" Elise yelled, pointing to Linda's hand. "I've installed cameras out here! They're recording all of this!"

Linda sharply looked at the roof's eaves for them.

In that instant, Elise took off.

Elise ran down the sidewalk, heart pumping. She dove across the street and into another neighbor's yard.

The center of her back twinged from an imagined impact of a bullet. She bobbed and weaved around trees and bushes, so Linda couldn't line her gun sites up, never checking to see if the woman was following.

Up ahead was the stop sign, and then the McGregor's house. She knew the woman was home. If she could just get there, she'd be safe. She'd call 911, Brad, and the entire calvary.

She jumped over a flower bed and squeezed between two rose bushes, ignoring the thorns as they tore her shirt. Out of breath, she ran up the porch and pounded on the front door.

Seconds passed. Elise dared a glance over her shoulder. No one was coming. She pounded again. *Please, please hurry!*

"Coming! Coming, my dear," a thin voice warbled through the door. Mrs. McGregor came into view, shuffling along in a bathrobe. She stared through the glass at Elise, her eyes squinting to focus. After a moment, a smile broke out across her face. "Oh. It's *you!*"

The old woman fiddled with the locks with agonizing slowness. Elise felt out of breath for a different reason now, more from anxiety then from running. *Come on. Come on.* She smiled encouragingly as she bounced on her toes.

Finally, the last lock clicked open and Mrs. McGregor opened the door. "I'm sorry it took so long. I'm a bit hard of hearing. How can I help you, dear?"

"Can I come in? Just for a moment?"

"Oh. Of course, dear. Come in." The little woman took a few steps back, barely raising her feet from the floor. Eventually, there was enough room for Elise to squeeze by.

Once inside, Elise shut the door and locked it, then peered out the window. Mrs. McGregor looked surprised but didn't say anything.

"Do you have a phone I could borrow? I need to make a quick phone call."

"Of course, dear. Right this way." Mrs. McGregor turned and led Elise into the living room. As if she'd been sleeping, her hair was flattened in the back in the shape of flower petals, the center held a patch of pink scalp. Elise followed behind her trying to calm down. *It's okay. I'm safe. I've got this.*

Mrs. McGregor pointed to an age-stained oak end table—the color of watery coffee. "Phone's right there, dear," she said.

"Thank you, Mrs. McGregor." Relief quickly dissipated as she realized she'd left everything back at the house—purse, keys, car door opened wide.

"Now, can I get you a cup of tea?"

Elise carefully worked her way around the older woman and over to the table. "Yes, that would be lovely."

"Oh, good. I finally get a chance to use my special china. Be right back, dear."

Sitting on a crocheted doily was an ancient phone. Elise picked up the receiver and stared down at the rotary dial. Hesitantly, she stuck her finger in the nine and rotated it through. She did the same two more times with the one and held the receiver to her ear.

Something was wrong. Where was the ringtone? She flicked the button up and down trying to get a connection. Nothing.

She bent down and located the phone wire, slowly tracing it down behind the couch. With a grunt, she scooted the couch out to see if the wire was plugged in.

Her mouth dropped open. The wire lay there, unplugged. It looked like the end was missing the connector, as if it had been sheared off.

What in the world? Had the wire been jerked too hard and the end come off? Who would leave an old woman in a house without a working phone?

Elise stood and rubbed her temples. What to do now? She pushed the couch back and started to pace the small room. Back and forth, back and forth. From the kitchen she could hear Mrs. McGregor puttering around. *She must have another one. Maybe a cell? Or a phone in another room?*

Her eye caught an interesting sight. Someone had stenciled calligraphy gracefully on the far wall. She walked over to read it, curious.

Though taken down the hole by gravity...

The rest of the words were hidden behind a large painting that rested on the top of a bookshelf. She cast a careful eye in the direction of the kitchen, where the spoon could still be heard hitting china—presumably stirring in a cup—and then tipped the painting forward just a bit, not daring to breathe in case she made noise.

The rest of the phrase came into sight, curling across the back wall and down the corner. *...the Hare shall welcome her into a dance. And there for a fortnight, a daydream and nightmare, they shall finally give their love a chance.*

She sucked in her breath. It wasn't the reference to falling down a hole that caught her breath; it was the stolen volume of *Alice in Wonderland* hidden behind the painting and staring straight in her face.

Shaking, she rested the painting back against the wall, her pulse thundering in her ears. *Dear Lord, how do I get out of this?* Her hands trembled as she glanced at the room's entrance.

Standing in it was Mrs. McGregor.

How long had she been standing there? Had she seen?

The old woman held two cups of tea in each hand. "Well, my dear. I'm awfully glad you decided to stop for a chat." She walked forward, her steps silent as the thick rubber of her slippers buffeted the sound. "Sit, sit!" the old lady insisted.

Elise turned and retreated to the rose-patterned arm chair. The upholstery was frayed and faded in the center. She clenched her hands to control her nerves, her mind spinning. Who was Mrs. McGregor? She played cribbage with Mrs. Perkins and Mrs. Campbell every Thursday. Elise had seen for herself when Mrs. McGregor would totter down toward Mrs. Perkins' house carrying some treat or another.

She accepted the cup from Mrs. McGregor and smiled, her smile feeling fragile and weak. *Can she tell? Does she know that I saw the book?* Her eyes were tempted to look at the painting again, where the book was hidden. *Don't do it.* She took a small sip of her tea and peeped at Mrs. McGregor over the rim of the cup.

"Lovely day, isn't it?" the old woman began. "I'd love for you to see my garden. I've been puttering about in it all week." She noticed the cup in Elise's hand. "Drink up, dear. This is my special Earl Grey."

"It really is," Elise answered, taking another big sip. She glanced at Mrs. McGregor to see if that satisfied her and placed the cup back in the saucer. The cup rattled so she rested it on her knee. "I've just heard from Brad, so I'm really going to have to cut our visit short." She gave what she'd hoped was a regretful grin. "But I'll be back next week to see your garden, if you have time."

"Oh, poo." The old woman's face fell. "And my grandson is on his way to meet you."

"Grandson?"

"Simon." The women cocked her head. "He said he's met you before."

"Really?" Elise thought hard about the name Simon. "I don't remember him. Was it at the bookstore?"

"I believe it...."

Just then heavy steps sounded against the house's old wooden steps leading to the porch. The front door jangled from being unlocked and then someone entered.

"Hello, Hello!" A deep male voice called as the door squeaked open. A dog shot through into the living room and stopped in front of Elise. "Bandersnatch, Dinah." Immediately, the friendly look dropped from the animal's face and her eyes became more alert. The hair between the German Shepherd's shoulders slowly rose.

The man walked over and scratched the dog's back. He gave Elise a big, open smile. "Fancy seeing you here, lovely."

Elise bit back a whimper as she looked up into his face. The face of someone she'd seen quite frequently as of late.

The face of a killer.

Chapter Twenty-Three

"Simon!" Mrs. McGregor said with excitement. "Sweetheart. So glad you made it. We have a guest."

The bald carpenter who'd built the escape room swung in the living room with easy steps. "Now Grandma, you know how I go by Harry now. Harry March," he winked at Elise.

Elise swallowed hard. How could she forget him? Forget how he'd nearly knocked his work buddy down the stairs for winking at her? How he was in the bookstore time and time again? How he'd smiled like he'd always known her.

Turning back to his grandma, Harry continued, "Did you give her the special drops?" He scratched the dog behind her ears.

"The vitamin drops? Yes, I sure did." Mrs. McGregor leaned forward toward Elise. "I hope you don't mind, dear. Simon gives them to me every night. Good for the health and you looked so piqued when you came to the door. I was worried."

"Harry, Grandma. Harry."

Elise looked at the tea. Already, the room was spinning.

"So, Grandma, I think Elise and I have some stuff to talk about. We need to catch up a bit. Do you mind?"

"Of course not, dear. I have my garden to tend to." The old woman stood unsteadily on her feet. She smiled at Elise. "I know you have to go soon, but maybe you could pop out and look at it for a minute?"

"I'd love to. How about right now?" Elise grabbed on to Mrs. McGregor's words.

"Not now." Harry snapped his fingers at the dog and Dinah inched closer. A low growl rumbled from the dog's throat. "Maybe next time, Grandma."

"Okay," the woman gave a sweet smile. "Next time, then." She shuffled from the room. A minute later, the back door could be heard closing.

"So," Harry began. "You came to see me. I knew you would."

"You...did?" The light from the windows seemed extra bright. She squinted and tried to look non-threatening.

"Drink your tea, Elise."

Elise raised the glass and Harry touched the bottom, helping to tip it up. She gulped it down, spilling a bit from the corners of her mouth.

"Good girl," he coaxed softly.

When the cup was empty, he took it from her and set it on the saucer. He looked at her, and his face flushed. "I just can't believe you're here. Finally, after all these years." He leaned over and took her hand. "You're so beautiful, just as you always have been."

Elise took a deep breath, feeling very relaxed. Her tongue felt thick and awkward. *Concentrate, Elise. Don't let your guard down.* "You've been waiting for me for a while."

"For a long while." He brought her hand to his mouth and kissed it. The light reflected off his bald head. She resisted a giggle that tried to bubble up.

"How long, Harry? Because I just met you."

His eyes narrowed. "You can stop that now."

"Stop...."

"Stop pretending. Now." Dinah heard the tone in his owner's voice and her chest rumbled in response.

Elise tried a different tactic. "Tell me about the time we met, Harry. What did you think when you first saw me?" She tucked a wisp of hair around her ear and smiled.

"You," he breathed out, "were beautiful. The most gorgeous creature I'd ever seen."

Elise waited. Harry looked down at his fingers and picked at one of his nails. A shy look came over his face. "I still remember the secret messages you sent me."

"Messages?"

"Painted on the mushroom."

Like a spinning kaleidoscope, the picture of the memory came together. She closed her eyes. He *did* know her. "The *Alice and Wonderland* play," she whispered.

"Yes. I knew you remembered. I saw it in your eyes that day in the bookstore. You were just as happy to see me as I was to see you. And then, when you mentioned the book, I knew what you wanted me to do." He scratched Dinah's neck, who still watched Elise fiercely. "But we had to keep it a secret. Keep it on the *down-low*." He emphasized the last words with a head bob.

"Your Grandma said you just came back. From treatment?" Keep him talking, her inner voice told her. But her rational mind was working as though through thick mud. She could barely formulate a sentence, let alone an escape plan. What was in those drops? Was it the same thing that Steve had ingested?

Was she about to die?

"Treatment." He rubbed his scalp. "Shock treatment. They wanted to stop the voices. They weren't real, they said. But I knew what they were. Memories and promises. It all came together when I saw you that day."

"Tell me more." The words came out slurred. She did her best to sit up straighter.

"It seemed like fate when I saw you there at the bookstore. I remembered how you wanted to be with me. And, I saw a way I could make that happen." His pupils

184

seemed to grow even larger. "Our own little world, Alice."

"My name's not Alice."

"Elise." He walked closer and brushed her hair off her shoulder. "Same thing."

"Why did you try to kill me on the horse, then?"

"You were a bad girl. You told the cops about my bugs. You needed to be punished." He studied her. "And now you're sleepy. I need to get you to bed."

He came close and wrapped his arm under her armpit. "Come on, sweetheart. Stand up." She stood and wobbled considerably. Her last course of action was to pretend she was way more drugged than she really was. A laugh tried to work its way out of her again. Pretend. Right.

The scent of old shoe-polish and stale cologne filled her nostrils, igniting the nausea from earlier. She swallowed hard.

"It's okay, my love. We've got this. We'll never be separated again. We're going to find our own wonderland." Carefully, Harry led her through the living room.

In the foyer, she saw the sunlight shining through front door's window and nearly whimpered.

"This way, little Alice." He guided her to the left.

She turned as if to go with him.

Tensed her muscles.

And broke free, racing for the door.

"Fetch!" Harry yelled.

She'd just reached the doorknob and struggled to turn it when Dinah was on her. Harry watched with cold eyes from the end of the hall as Dinah clamped her teeth down on Elise's thigh. She cried out, still trying to open the lock. All these locks. Her hands felt like flippers as she batted them against the bolts.

"Dodo!" The dog released her, leaving a bloody trail on her pants. Harry approached her and grabbed her by the hair. "Such a naughty girl," he hissed in her ear. Yanking her by the hair, he dragged her down the hall, ignoring when she stumbled.

There was a door at the end that looked like it had once been painted shut. An eye-hook lock hung from the top of it. He roughly yanked the door open to reveal a set of stairs.

"Down the rabbit hole you go," he said, dragging her down the stairs.

"No, please. No!" she yelled as she was forced into the dark basement.

"My little Alice," he yanked her across the cold floor to a cot and forced her to sit. "You must stay here until I'm ready to make you queen."

Chapter Twenty-Four

Harry flung her onto a cot. He held up a finger in warning. "Be good, or I'll send Dinah down the stairs to handle you."

Elise's leg throbbed and she nodded. Fear fought with her dizziness.

"You'll see, sweetheart. This will all work out." He whistled and Dinah ascended the stairs ahead of him. Harry climbed after her, hesitating at the top. "If not, the Jabberwocky will come."

Cold chills ran down Elise's back. "I'll be good," she whispered.

"I'll be down later with some food." He didn't look back as he shut the door. She heard the lock fasten.

Still feeling dizzy, Elise looked around. A bit of light filtered through a tiny window near the top of the ceiling, a window far too small for her to fit through. But it gave her enough light to see her surroundings, and for that she was grateful.

The air smelled musty from mold and decades-old dust. It didn't seem like anyone had been down here in a long while, other than to recently move in a cot. She touched the surface of the cot, her face squeezing in fear. Since it was new, it meant he'd planned to bring her here all along.

She shifted on the cot, causing a shard of pain to fly up her leg. Grimacing, she pulled down her pants to check the wound.

Blood oozed from five puncture marks, but seemed to have slowed down. Bruising caused a dark red circle around the wound. Her eyes closed in pain as she eased her pants back up. There was nothing she could do about it now.

She tried to stand, but the room whirled and immediately knocked her back on her butt. Luckily the cot was there to catch her. Hot tears squeezed out of her eyes as she held her throbbing head.

The basement was dank and cold. The concrete floor was covered in a river of cracks, and two metal pillars held up the beams to the first floor. In the back corner sat a complete kitchen counter complete with a 1970's style Formica, obviously replaced long ago.

The cot she sat on had a pillow and an old quilt. She held the quilt to her face and sniffed. It smelled of fresh laundry soap. Just that simple normal thing nearly unwound her. *No one knows where I am. I'm never going to get out of here.*

Stop it! You are in no position to indulge in self-pity. You're strong, smart. Think your way out.

How do you think your way out when there's only one way out? Heaviness descended on her. She couldn't tell if it was the drugs or hopelessness.

She rested her head back on the pillow and tried to assess the situation.

Harry remembers me from high school. Scrunching her face in concentration, she tried to remember him. But, no matter how hard she tried, she couldn't place him, maybe because of his missing hair. Possibly, he was taller and more filled out now. She thought back to the time she tried out for the play. It hadn't been a good experience. The hardest part had been the horrible embarrassment of singing in front of everyone and still not making the part. Even worse, they'd given her the consolation prize of working on the set.

The stage manager had handed her a bucket of paint and ushered her over to a big mushroom. "Paint it," one of the stage hand's directed. And so she did. No one had bothered to explain what their expectation was, so she'd done swirls and diamonds.

He'd said it was a secret code. What did he think she'd said? And, how had he even seen the mushroom?

Elise covered her mouth with her hands as the realization sunk in. Of course. Harry had played the caterpillar. She remembered a skinny kid, four years younger than she was, pretending to smoke the hookah pipe. He'd acted so goofy that she'd teased him by asking if he really *was* smoking something.

She remembered the last day when they told her they wouldn't need her anymore. He'd come up to her, looking so bashful that his acne-covered face blushed to an even deeper red. "You're my queen of hearts," he'd whispered.

Didn't she hear that he'd left without finishing the school year? She couldn't remember, her already fuzzy brain protesting at how hard it was being made to work right now.

The pillow felt softer by the second under her head. *Just give me a minute. I'll figure all of this out a minute.*

❖ ❖ ❖

She woke up with a start. The light from the window was gone. Her heart beat hard as the thick blackness of the basement seem to suffocate her. *Breathe. Just breathe. You're going to be okay.*

Slowly, she sat up in the bed. Her tongue felt like a carpet and she was dying of thirst. Her head gave a sharp throb but settled down as she stayed upright.

As she lowered her feet, they bumped against something on the floor. Immediately, she drew them back up. Her shoes were missing. *Don't think about that right now. Just figure out what you touched.* Cautiously, she lowered one foot and felt around. Metal scraped against the basement floor.

She reached out with her hand to feel what it was.

A metal bucket. Maybe to relieve herself in?

Raising her hand, she bumped into something else and it clattered. Blindly, she reached out again, this time her hand finding a metal edge. She traced it around to discover it was a TV tray.

Suddenly, she noticed a new scent in the air. Yeasty. Bread maybe. Had food been brought down? Was there something to drink?

Almost without control, she felt around on the tray, nearly crying out with gratitude when she discovered a cup. She brought it to her mouth and took a sip, trying to be cautious. Water. Her thirst took over and she drank it with greedy gulps, no longer caring if it was poisoned.

The cup was half-way empty when she reluctantly placed it back on the tray. Gently, she felt around some more, her fingers jerking away when they touched something soft. She reached again and discovered a sandwich.

Her stomach growled as she brought it to her mouth. She took a bite—peanut butter and jelly—and chewed slowly. Her excitement dropped at the vision of Harry standing over her watching her sleep, and her blood ran cold.

She swallowed and closed her eyes. *Don't think about it. Just eat and drink and figure this out.*

After a few more bites, her mind went back to Harry. Who was he?

He was a carpenter.

A carpenter.

Like a flash, she saw how this all played out. He'd been the one who designed the Escape Room. He hadn't cared about who he hurt or killed. He just wanted to create a distraction to steal the book. He'd known how to copy her key.

She shook her head as she remembered the construction crew at the horse ranch. He'd heard her talk about riding horses on her birthday through the bug in her house, and he'd been waiting there that day. And she bet the entire bookstore was bugged. He probably listened to everything she said, including when she talked to the Detectives, Dave, and Brad.

He knew when she was at work and when she went home.

A white truck flickered in her imagination. Was he the one at the neighbor's house every day? Had he been watching her that closely?

This is crazy.

No crazier than being trapped in a basement by someone calling you Alice.

Goosebumps crawled up her arm as fear made another concentrated attack.

Grabbing her head, she squeezed her temples. *No. No. No. This isn't going to help. Don't let your imagination have control.*

She took a deep breath, held it for seven seconds, and back-tracked.

He's a construction worker. Specifically, he's a carpenter.

He loves *Alice and Wonderland* and knows every line and phrase.

She thought about the dog. What was it that Harry said to get the dog to guard her? She'd been so out of it then, she could barely remember.

There had to be something she could work with here. Just as soon as it got to be light.

I might not have the chance to wait that long....

If it's daylight then Harry would have to go to work. Would he leave her there?

No, he wouldn't.

She had to figure a way out now.

A faint glow of moonlight filtered through the tiny window. Not enough to really see by. But she had to try.

She stood and carefully walked across the basement, barely raising her feet to feel around. Thirty-five steps. Her leg throbbed as she felt the cinder blocks that made the other wall and turned to walk back.

What was that? She heard police sirens. Brad! He was looking for her! Blue and red flashing lights spilled for a brief second through the basement's window as the police cars drove by. She limped across the floor to climb on the cot and pressed her face against the dirty window. *I'm right here!* She slammed her fist on the glass.

The glass didn't even shudder.

Brokenhearted, she slunk back down to the cot. Could she break the glass and scream for help before Harry heard her? It was an option, but not her best one. Her fist wouldn't work. She looked around for something hard enough that could be used.

Pillow. Blanket. Plastic cup and plate. Tin metal table and bucket.

She covered her face. *Dear God, please get me out of here.*

Tears burned her eyes at the thought of Brad. And Lucy! *Please, please, please.*

Chapter Twenty-Five

Loud scraping woke her up. Elise groaned. How had she fallen asleep again? She didn't know, but the fogginess in her brain had cleared. Her mind felt sharp and ready for action.

Boots thumping on the stairs made her roll over. She quickly sat up and straightened her shirt as Harry appeared. Dinah came down by his side, the animal's hair raising along her back at the sight of Elise.

"Breakfast!" Harry smiled as if he were preparing for his wedding day. "How are you doing, beautiful?"

She watched him cautiously. In his hands, he held a steaming bowl and a large plastic cup. Her hands immediately began reaching for the glass as if they had a will of their own.

"I brought you some breakfast," he said, setting the dishes down on the tray. "Oatmeal and some H2O." He glanced at the empty plate. "I see you found dinner last night. Good."

He moved to sit next to her on the cot. She scooted away and grabbed the cup. "Thank you," she murmured, her mouth dry. She took a few slow swallows as he leaned in close. He sniffed her hair and she struggled not to shudder.

"Even being down here doesn't tarnish your looks," his words breathed against her cheek. She fought to hold her composure.

"So!" he said, sitting straighter. "I have a plan. Would you like to hear it?"

She nodded.

His gaze flicked to the movie tray. "Eat. Eat." He laughed. "It won't make you grow small here."

Biting her lip, she reached for the bowl. Milk sat on top of the oatmeal and held a greasy sheen. She took a small bite.

"Mmm," she said, hoping it would appease him.

He seemed pleased. Crossing his legs, he rested his hands on his knee.

"So, like I was saying. I have a plan. I think I have a potential buyer for the book. Can you believe the serendipity of this book bringing us together? Bringing both of our dreams to fruition?"

Elise nodded and smiled.

"Afterward it's sold, we're going to use the money to get away from here. I've already found a house. Very secluded, by a lake. No one will ever bother us again. We can live just like you intended. The White King and Queen." His eyes shone feverishly.

Terror filled Elise's heart.

"But for now," he continued. "I need to make sure you stay a good girl. So I'm going to need to tie you." He pulled out a bandana from his pocket. "Gag you. It's for your own good. You'll see."

He rolled the bandana and placed it in her mouth then tied it tight behind her head. His fingers beckoned for her hands. Holding back a whimper, she held them out to him. He pulled them behind her back and crossed them together, then fastened them with a zip tie.

"Now, I'll be watching to make sure you do as your told. And just for good measure, I'm leaving Dinah down here to guard you." His eyes took a hard glint as he studied her. Then, with almost a hyper energy, he turned to the dog. "Hungry Dinah? I haven't fed her today, you see. She'll have to earn her dinner."

He looked back at Elise. "You haven't behaved very well, but you can prove you will now. It's all going to work out. We're going to be so happy, you'll see."

Grabbing the back of her neck, he drew her close. She couldn't help resisting him. Not put off, he pressed his mouth against hers as if the gag wasn't there. After a long kiss, he released her with a satisfied look. "I'll see you tonight, my queen. We have lots to talk about."

He sprang up and patted the dog on the head, before looping a leash around the bottom of the stair banister. He snapped the other end onto the dog's collar.

"You two have a good day now!" He waved and jogged up the stairs with a happy whistle. The door made a click as he locked it.

Dinah looked at her and growled, low and dangerous.

Elise took slow and deep breaths. She could feel the fear creeping in, threatening to make her lose her mind.

Upstairs, she could hear footsteps, and then the front door slammed. That had to be him.

A creepy feeling crawled up her spine. She looked along the ceiling but didn't see cameras. Maybe he was bluffing about watching her, but it didn't matter. It was now or never. She needed to figure out how to get out of this mess.

First thing's first. She wiggled on the cot until she was able to get her hands in front of her. The plastic band cut a white indentation into her skin.

She glanced at the dog, who growled at the movement. How long was that leash? Mentally, she tried to measure it, finally deciding the dog couldn't reach her if she walked as close to the wall as possible. It was a gamble, and there was only one way to be sure.

As she stood up, the dog charged. Elise flinched and a cry shot out of her throat, stifled by the gag. But the dog was just shy of reaching her. Slowly, Elise made her way to the other side of the basement as Dinah followed her at the length of her leash, canines flashing.

Limping, Elise made it to the old kitchen unit. She ran her thumb against the old Formica. It was sharp on the unfinished side that had faced the wall. Clenching her hands into fists, she ran the plastic band over the edge. Over and over, like she was starting a fire. At the same time, she pulled against the band, trying to stretch it thin.

Sweat formed on her neck as she scraped at the zip tie. The skin around her wrist was raw and red. Droplets of blood fell to the floor. Still she sawed the band.

Snap! Finally, it came free. She untied the sodden gag from her mouth and fell to her knees with relief.

Dinah huffed and growled even more ferociously at the movement.

After catching her breath, she dabbed her wrists with the handkerchief and walked carefully back to the cot. The dog settled down as soon as Elise sat back on the bed.

One problem's solved. But you're still trapped. Take your time, but think.

She wrapped the handkerchief around her knuckles and stood up on the cot to examine the tiny window. *This has to be the last resort. I might be able to break it and yell for help, but there's a good chance there'd be no one around to hear me.*

Sighing, she collapsed back onto the cot.

A chunk of crust sat on the floor. Something that must have dropped from the night before. She looked at the dog.

Immediately at catching her gaze, the dog growled.

She thought about Harry. His mannerisms. His habits.

His worship of *Alice in Wonderland.*

An idea floated in her mind. The dog's name was from *Alice in Wonderland.* And what was that command? She tried to remember.

"Dinah, Tweedle Dee!"

The dog tipped her head as her bottom thumped to the ground.

She's sitting. Is she doing it by that command?

"Tweedle Dum."

The dog's ears perked but she didn't move.

"Dodo!"

Dinah jumped up and raced toward her, barking. She flinched as the German Shepherd was jerked to a stop by the leash. The stair railing creaked under the dog's force. How had that worked when Harry had said it?

"Tweedle Dee!" she yelled again, flinging her arm over her eyes.

The barking stopped. Elise peered to see the dog sitting. But the shepherd's lip quivered over bared teeth.

Elise threw the scrap of her sandwich toward the animal. The dog never waved in its stare at her. She ran her hands through her hair and pulled.

Nothing's working!

One word. One word had to work. Keep thinking.

"Alice," she commanded. The dog didn't move.

"Mad Hatter." No movement.

She rattled off a succession of what she could remember, "White Queen. Cards. Red Queen. Red King. Caterpillar! Cheshire Cat. March Hare."

The dog gave her no reaction to any of these.

In desperation, she yelled the one name that Harry had threatened her with the night before. "Jabberwockey!"

The dog laid down and rested her muzzle on her paws.

A tiny flutter of excitement rose in Elise's chest. Did it work? Was that real? She stood up and tentatively took a step closer. The dog didn't move.

She had one chance. One chance to make it past the dog. And if the dog attacked, she'd have no escape.

Elise grabbed the pillow and stuffed it under her shirt. She wound the quilt around her legs like a skirt and tied it. Her arms felt vulnerable, as did her face.

She grabbed the TV tray and folded it to resemble an awkward shield.

The dog watched her, eyebrows twitching.

"Jabberwocky," she said again.

Dinah whined.

It was now or never.

She slowly limped toward the stairs, keeping the tray between her and the dog. Dinah watched for as long as she could, but never raised her head.

Elise reached the stairs and backed up them, one by one. What would she find at the top? She had no idea.

Mrs. McGregor?

Or Harry.

She tried the knob and discovered it locked. Well, she'd suspected that. Using the tray as a shoulder pad, she smashed into the door as hard as she could.

The door creaked. Quickly, she smashed it again. She was not going to stay here. NO! NO! NO! With each no, she ran into the door.

The final push broke the flimsy eye-hook lose and the door busted free. She tumbled into the hallway and nearly fell. Without looking to see who was around, she ran for the front door.

She unfastened the door, lock after lock after lock. Flinging the door open with a sob, she hobbled out.

Her bare feet slapped against the pavement. She ran for the house directly across the street and never looked back.

Chapter Twenty-Six

— Twenty-Four Hours Later —

Elise walked out onto the overlook and gazed out at the bluff. White-capped waves looked like swimming geese against the blue of Angel Lake far below. The wind pulled at her hair. She liked to think that the breeze had traveled from some exotic place far away, rather than just start with a spit and a turn in her little town.

Yesterday. Her leg throbbed under a bandage of gauze. Her heart still felt the effects of icy fingers of terror.

But he's not going to win. I was stronger and I won.

After running across the street, her frantic knocks on the neighbor's door brought a very confused woman to the door. Elise had barely been able to ask for help, so terrified that Harry was right behind her. Even though she must have looked crazed, the woman had ushered her in and ten minutes later the police, along with Brad, were there.

Mrs. McGregor had known where Harry was working that day, and the police honed in on him at his newest job. He'd been insulted when the officers called him Simon, and apparently began berating them about his great mental prowess. Later, the officers recovered the *Alice and Wonderland* book and the bottle of 'special vitamins' that Detective Sloan felt forensics would prove contributed to Steve's death. Another interesting piece of evidence discovered in Harry's work truck was a cigar tube that was filled with hat pins.

Harry now sat in jail.

Elise's hair blew across her mouth and she raised a hand to free it from her lips. She gazed out at the water again, the little ripples growing bigger as the waves picked up.

A lone figure picked his way across the beach below. She shaded her eyes to study him. Lean, dark hair. He looked up towards her and her heart leaped.

Brad.

He saw her and waved. Then he turned and gazed down the length of the bluff. In the next moment, he was running and out of sight.

What the heck? Where did he go?

Elise leaned as close as she dared to peer over the edge of the bluff, but he was gone. As she stood back, she gathered her hair to the nape of her neck. The grass blew around her in whispers.

She thought about the conversation late last night—or was it early this morning? She'd been lying in Brad's arms, not ever wanting ever to move again. Letting his strength soothe away the fear of her night in the basement.

He'd whispered that he would have found her. He'd never stop looking. That he was so proud of her.

"So proud. You are so strong. I love you. Love you so much."

She'd let his words fill her. His warmth surrounded her as she relaxed and breathed in the clean scent of his cologne, his natural smell.

After a while, she shifted to look into his eyes. "I was right to be worried about the neighbors. I just was focused on the wrong ones."

He smoothed her hair from her face and kissed her. "Linda and Seth spent the entire night looking for you. Linda felt terrible that she'd scared you. You did too good of a job getting away from her."

"I thought she had a gun."

"She had a letter. You couldn't have known this, but she's Lucy's second cousin. She'd been trying to find her for months, and finally tracked her here. That's why they rented the house. They've been trying to check you out. See if Lucy was really safe."

"Why didn't Lucy recognize her?"

"I don't know, hun. I think they mentioned that they were on her father's side. Maybe they never met."

"What does this mean for Lucy?"

"I'm not sure. But we'll figure all of this out. We'll get through this." He drew his fingers along her jaw and down her neck. "You were right to be wary about the construction truck at their house, though."

"Was it Harry?" Her skin prickled.

"Yeah. When he saw them move in, he offered the landlord free renovating services. He said it was because he wanted a reference for future business. He was updating their kitchen."

"And Lucy?"

"She's fine. She's going to be fine. And so are you." The moment melted with more love.

Flowers brushed against Elise's leg under her dress. She picked one—a daisy—and began pulling the petals.

He loves me. He loves me not. He loves me.

Suddenly, there was Brad's dark head again, making his way up a hidden trail. His eyes were on the ground as he picked his way along the path.

"Hey, handsome!" she called. He looked up, beaming when he spotted her. His steps sped up.

When he reached her, he wrapped her in his arms with a promise to never let her go. He kissed her once, twice, his lips trailing down her neck until she giggled and pulled away.

"Thank you for meeting me here," he said, running his hand down her back.

"How's Lucy? Lavina has her?" Elise asked.

Brad took in a deep breath, as though there was something else he wanted to say, then seemed resigned at the direction Elise needed the conversation to go. "She's doing good. Last I saw her, she had four bags of clothes and pink hair."

"Pink hair?"

"I'm kidding." He leaned in and nuzzled her neck again. "But she's fine and safe. And now, this is our time."

He stepped back and gently brushed her wind-tossed hair from her face. His eyes were dark as they studied hers. "I've waited my entire life for this, and I'm not waiting one second more. It's time to give you your birthday present." His hands raised a line of goosebumps where they stroked down her arms until they met her own. He gathered them together and brought them to his lips to kiss.

Elise looked up, shaken when she saw his eyes fill with tears.

Slowly, he dropped to one knee.

"Brad!" she exclaimed, his name catching in her throat.

He reached into his pocket and brought out a tiny box. *The box.*

Heart pounding in her chest, Elise's breath caught in her throat. This was happening. Really happening.

"Elise, my love, you say that you need me, that you see me as your hero. But you've got it all wrong. You're *my* hero. You are so strong and so beautiful- inside and out. You have more heart than anyone I've ever known. I love you in every way a man can love a woman. You're my best friend, my lover, my better half. I can hardly wait to see what life has in store for us." Elise clasped her hands over her mouth, willing her trembling legs to hold her up. His hazel eyes crinkled in the corners with a smile as he opened the box. "And I know it will be amazing with you by my side."

Nestled inside, an antique ring's diamond sparkled in a rose setting, with tiny slivers of green emeralds for leaves. He took it out, then looked up at her. His expression was so eager and hopeful and Elise felt everything fall into place.

"Elise, will you make me the happiest man in the world and marry me?"

She couldn't speak, the knot in her throat was so big. She nodded, tears falling down her face as he slid the ring on her finger. She smiled then, so hard and wide it hurt and he leaped up, catching her up in his arms. They held one another tightly, and Elise knew she had finally come home as his mouth crushed hers.

This man! This man is mine!

Many minutes later, he grabbed her hand and they slowly walked back to the trail.

"I have a lot more plans for the day if you're up for them," Brad said, going slow for her injured leg. "But I wanted to propose to you up here, overlooking Angel Lake. Our place. Where it all began."

She looked out at the water and squeezed his hand. "It's perfect."

"So, what kind of wedding do you want?" he asked, his eyes twinkling. "Lots of flowers and guests?"

"I just want everyone there that I love, my friends and my family."

"Oh, trust me. They're all going to be there."

"Even Mr. G?" Elise smiled.

"He's coming. He's offering a free concert as his wedding present to us." He grinned. "Your mom's going to pass out when she sees him."

"My mom? How about me." She nudged Brad in the arm. "He's still kind of hot."

"You're giving me a complex. How can I ever compete?"

Elise grinned and looped her arms around his shoulders. Smiling up at his face, she traced his cheek with her thumb. "You're kind of hot, too, Mr. Carter."

"Flattery will get you everywhere, Mrs. Carter."

The End

Thank you for reading the Tempting Taste of Danger

Other books in the series-
The Sweet Taste of Murder
The Bitter Taste of Betrayal
The Sour Taste of Suspicion
The Honeyed Taste of Deception

43299611R00132

Made in the USA
San Bernardino, CA
13 July 2019